Savage Pilgrims

by Susan Tekulve

3/28/13

For Alyson,
With admiration for
your talent. It was
a _real_ pleasure to meet
you,

SERVING HOUSE BOOKS

All Best,
Susan

Savage Pilgrims

ISBN: 978-0-9825462-0-8

Serving House Books logo by Barry Lereng Wilmont

Published by Serving House Books

www.servinghousebooks.com

First Edition

"One must learn to love, and go through a good deal of suffering to get to it, and the journey is always towards the other soul."

—D.H. Lawrence (1885-1930)

For Rick and Hunter

Contents

Acknowledgements

"Drawing the Body," *Beloit Fiction Journal*
"My Mother's War Stories," *Denver Quarterly*
"Pilgrimage to the Black Madonna," *North Dakota Quarterly*
"The Worst Thing I'll Ever Do To You," *Emrys*
"The Flight Patterns of Birds," *Connecticut Review*
"Tarantata," *Clackamas Literary Review*
"Stoics," *Clackamas Literary Review*

Susan Tekulve's short fiction collection, *My Mother's War Stories,* was published by Winnow Press (Austin, Texas). Her nonfiction, stories and poems have appeared in *Shenandoah, New Letters, Best New Writing 2007, The Indiana Review, Denver Quarterly, Puerto del Sol, Prairie Schooner, Beloit Fiction Journal, Crab Orchard Review, The Literary Review, Web Del Sol, Black Warrior Review,* and *The Kansas City Star.* She has been awarded scholarships from the Bread Loaf Writers' Conference and the Sewanee Writers' Conference. An associate professor of English at Converse College in South Carolina, she is completing a novel.

Gabriel

After Botticelli's "L'Annunciazione di Cestello," 1489-1490

It was easier to tell the biters and fornicators
their days would not be long.
Now he must crouch. Amphibious wings backswept, he must carry
those troublesome lilies, Eve's tears
upturned, surrendering to twilight.
His face aged by knowing
what he must tell, he raises
one watchful hand. Mary tilts
away, her red gown streaming
down her immaculate body.
Eyes and mouth shut, she pauses
him with one hand
as if to say not this, not now, not yet.

Drawing the Body

My mother went to a strip bar when she was eight months pregnant with my little sister. That Saturday night, she and my father attended mass at Our Lady of the Rosary church so they wouldn't have to go in the morning. Then they picked up Mr. Gunn, a family friend who was divorcing and needed some cheering up, and took him across the Ohio River to Greg Smitz Rendezvous, a gentlemen's club in downtown Newport. Some time after midnight, my parents' voices pulled me from a sound sleep into the butler's pantry; they were playing poker with sugar-coated almonds in the kitchen. I overheard my mother say that the drinks at the bar weren't watered down and you could get a square meal for a decent price. Mr. Gunn said he couldn't believe she'd wrapped her hand around his fist when he offered a twenty dollar bill to a stripper for a table dance. My father asked what in Christ's holy heaven made her want to dance on a table before her husband and her unborn baby's godfather, not to mention the racketeers who looked on from private booths in the club's darkest corners.

"We'll save that twenty dollars for the baby's education," she replied, slapping her cards on the table.

"I love pregnant women," Mr. Gunn said.

My mother was more beautiful when she was expecting. She transformed a sleeveless nightgown into a dress by wearing it with a string of pearls. Her thick black hair curled wildly around her face. She stopped dieting, allowing herself a potato *and* bread with her meals, which must have put her in a bold mood that night. I imagined her kicking off her sandals, slowly pulling her maternity hose down her legs and wrapping them like a stole around my father's neck. She must have stepped up on a chair to get onto the table. Rolling her hips, she swayed between Mr. Gunn and my father, hitching her thin dress above her knees, tossing her hair. She might have slipped her dress off the right shoulder, then the left, as though she were unwrapping a gift. Perhaps the baby shifted, its movements sending a shock wave that swept her off balance. She teetered dangerously above the two men until my father caught her below the arms, safely lifting her to the ground.

Pregnancy made my mother unpredictable and benevolent. She adopted family acquaintances who were in dire straights—divorcees, drinkers, ex-priests—calling her kind acts "my savior's complex." Because Mrs. Gunn was paying a lawyer for a no-contest divorce and moving the kids back to Georgia after school let out, Mr. Gunn needed a good deal of my mother's comfort that spring. One minute, he sipped Cold Duck from a coffee cup while he and my parents played poker. The next, he slapped his cards out on the table, saying, "That's it. I'm out. I've got nothing left." He disappeared into our living room to lie on the hardwoods without a pillow, his hand-carved cane lying beside him. I was never allowed in that room. Window-lit, with polished pine floors and a walnut piano, the room held Queen Anne furniture covered with clean bed sheets, off limits except on Easter and Christmas. My mother always excused herself to get my father another martini and to cover Mr. Gunn with an afghan. Then, she made a guilty phone call to Mrs. Gunn: "It's not that we're taking sides, Barbara," she said. "We still want both you and Marty to be the baby's godparents."

Barbara Gunn directed our church choir on Sundays, waving her left hand in the air while she played "Prepare ye the way of the Lord" on the pipe organ. My classmates at Our Lady of the Rosary school often joked that if Mary's mother lifted the other arm, she'd fly away. My father said she was divorcing Mr. Gunn because he loved women *too* much. My mother said that was only part of the problem. Mr. Gunn had survived polio as a boy, and his grateful parents had encouraged him to become a priest. Then he'd dropped out of seminary school to become an artist and father four children. My mother believed Mrs. Gunn thought she'd fallen in love with the hand of God but found herself married to a house painter who drank too much and told dirty jokes to other men's wives. Over the phone, my mother confessed to Mrs. Gunn that she'd had two stillbirths and one gangrenous ovary removed before this pregnancy, and she believed that an ex-priest and a choir director—even if they were divorcing—would give her the blessed insurance she needed to get through this one.

Before our parents left for the strip club that night, Mr. Gunn's daughter, Mary, and I agreed to indulge in our Lenten sacrifices. I'd given up potato chips with hopes that I'd drop a few pounds and make Robbie Shoemaker fall in love with me. Mary had given up profanities. Her three older brothers taught her jokes that could make a sailor blush.

"What's six inches long, with a big head and every woman loves it?" Mary said. My father's forehead reddened as he slipped a shawl over my mother's shoulders and opened the front door for her.

"I don't know, dear," he said.

"A hundred dollar bill," Mary said.

"Mea culpa," Mr. Gunn laughed. "Remind me to wash that kid's mouth out when we get home."

Mary had gotten away with telling dirty jokes since the divorce began two months before. A redhead with a figure my parents called "womanly," she passed for a sixteen year old though she was only twelve, and her father gave her the car keys after he'd had too much to drink. When he picked her up after school every afternoon, Mr. Gunn brought Mary gold-posted earrings or a bag of tea cookies. Once, he'd given us both learn-to-draw sketchbooks, saying, "I'm sorry, Anna. I feel like I've failed you too."

As soon as the headlights of my father's green Torino dimmed out of the driveway, Mary flipped off the T.V. and ran into the living room.

"Let's play church," she said.

"We're not allowed in here," I said, but Mary went into the pantry to get the grape juice and potato chips.

"Here's the body and blood of Christ," she said eagerly.

Mary had dropped out of piano lessons right after Christmas, so she played "We Three Kings" over and over for the processional while I acted as priest. I skipped right through the gospel and homily to the Acts of Contrition, saying a quick Lord's Prayer and blessing the gifts.

"This is my body, which shall be given up for you," I said, placing

13

the greasy wafer on her tongue. After Mary played three more rounds of "Oh, Holy Night," I flopped onto the couch with the chip canister in my lap and ate hungrily.

"I know why Rosie wanted to go to that strip bar tonight," Mary said. Recently, she'd begun calling our parents by their first names.

"Why?"

"Marty says it's because some men become less attracted to their pregnant wives," she said. "He says Albert needs a little help in the bedroom."

"That's not true," I said.

"The sad fact is that men are crude animals. They'll look at a woman's tits and ass long before they ever get around to her face."

According to Mary, the world was populated by the two types of men who went to strip bars. My father was the type who sat quietly and watched, drawing sociological conclusions about the strippers. "She's had a Cesarean," he'd say. "She must have children." Mr. Gunn was the type who paid for his favorite stripper's drinks so that she would sit down and talk to him. I imagined my mother, father and Mr. Gunn sitting around a table in the sexual darkness, music pounding in their stomachs, a dancer at Mr. Gunn's elbow where Mary's mother might have sat.

"Mark my word," Mary said. "When Rosie and Albert get home tonight, they'll be bumping the uglies."

"I don't understand the big deal about looking at a woman's naked body," I said. "It's only the flesh."

Mary took out her sketch pad. Like her father, she was always pulling out pencil and paper at sudden, inspired moments. The directions in our Learn-to-Draw books taught you how to create elephants and horses by sketching a proportionate arrangement of triangles. Then you filled in the flesh and fur over the shapes. Neither of us had gotten past animals and still lifes, but Mary reasoned that the human body could be drawn the same way.

"Take off your clothes and let me draw you," she said. When I hesitated, she taunted. "It's only your flesh."

I pulled my jeans and underwear down to my ankles, but then

14

I remembered that my shoes were still on. I took my time undoing the laces before kicking them off and lifting my sweatshirt. Mary licked the end of her charcoal pencil and looked straight at me, holding the pencil up between us. "For scale," she said, going to work, all business, her rough sketches falling to the floor like ladies' white slips.

"My dad says the best time to have your nude portrait drawn is before you turn thirty," Mary said, holding the pencil up again. I crossed and uncrossed my arms over my chest and hopped from one foot to the other to keep warm. How could anyone stand still for this?

"Stop fidgeting," she said. "Hold it right there."

Mary wanted to stay with her father in Ohio and become an artist. Mr. Gunn still drew a little, and when she was at his new apartment, she stole his crumpled-up charcoal studies and took them home to squirrel beneath her canopied bed. I secretly wanted to be a harem dancer, but I was too ashamed of my body. My father frequently pinched my sturdy thighs and thick arms, saying, "Husky. I like you like this." My mother consoled me with articles from ladies' fashion magazines.

"If you can't wrap your middle finger and thumb around your wrist, you're big boned," she said. "There's nothing you can do about it."

For as long as I could remember, love and heartache had been linked to our family's bathroom scale. Instead of visiting her two babies' graves, my mother mourned her postpartum weight. After each pregnancy, she'd stand on the scale in front of the mirror for hours, brushing her hair until thick clumps of it fell into the bathroom sink. Once, I gave her my report card to sign, and she blotted her lipstick on it, went back into the bathroom and closed the door.

I ran into the master bedroom to explore the mysteries behind the paneled headboard of my parents' mahogany bed, where my father kept an ashtray I'd made out of clay, filling it with pocket change, and my mother kept a sewing kit and a diaphragm, curved like an oyster's shell and snapped into a plastic case. I didn't know what it was. I stretched it, tossed it across the room like a Frisbee and poked holes in it with pearl-headed pins from her sewing kit. I fell asleep on the floor outside the bathroom door waiting for her to come out again. When the door finally swung open, she stood in baggy satin underwear and a stained nursing bra. I knew her body better than my own. I'd wished for one like it, praying for a narrow waist and thighs that didn't rub or chafe. The only evidence of motherhood was a pouch of flesh below her navel.

"I'm all stretched out from these babies, but I feel so empty," she'd said. "I feel like a human light bulb."

"Proportion is the hardest thing," Mary said, closing her sketch pad. "I must have gotten you at some bad angles."

"Let's take a peek," I said.

Mary's drawing looked like a failed geometry test; two small, lopsided circles for breasts, a triangle for pubic hair, a huge globe for a belly, two bulging ovals for thighs. Faceless and handless, with a mass of black frizzy hair over the round head, it was the ugliest human being I'd ever seen.

"The face and hands are the most difficult," Mary said. "Now I know why there are all those famous statues with their heads and arms missing."

"They lost them in earthquakes and wars," I said, my face burning. "They didn't start off that way."

"The Venus De Milo did," she said, looking back at the drawing. "The truth is it's a reasonable likeness. That's why you're upset."

"You'll never be an artist," I yelled, grabbing the drawing out of her hands.

Ashamed of my nakedness, I tore one of the bed sheets from the couch, wrapped it around my torso and took the drawing into the bathroom. I searched the linen closet for the red candlesticks my mother used for power outages and Christmas Eve. I lit one and held the drawing over the candle flame, beginning to see a distorted resemblance to myself—the small, uneven breasts, the round stomach, the frizzy dark hair. The burnt paper curled and flapped against the porcelain sink like black wings and the red candle wax dripped down the commode.

Instead of making love that night, my parents argued over hands of five card draw while I sat on the floor of the butler's pantry, listening. After

16

Mr. Gunn went home, they disputed the circumstances surrounding his divorce.

"He shouldn't have told her," my father said.

"Maybe he wanted her to help him stop," my mother said.

"He had an obligation to protect her from all that."

"You mean he should have lied?"

"I could understand him wanting to tell her about the first one. The first affair could have been a mistake. But the others? That was something she didn't need to know. He raised it to a new level of cruelty by telling her that."

"Maybe he couldn't live with himself any longer."

"If you want to stay married—if you want to see your children on a daily basis—you keep it to yourself. You tell a priest about it, but no one else. You live with your guilt."

"But he didn't tell her about all of them—"

"You don't tell, Rosie," my father warned.

My mother drifted into my room a few hours later. She'd taken off her pearls and nursing bra, but still wore the nightgown. I could see her swollen figure beneath the filmy crepe.

"Anna?" When I didn't answer, she climbed into my twin bed. "Sometimes I think there is too much of me."

"You're pregnant," I said, squeezing against the wall to make more room for her. "You're supposed to be big."

"No, what I mean is sometimes I feel like it must take more than a house and your father to fill me up."

"I'm never getting pregnant," I said.

"Sure you will," she said.

"No," I said. "I won't."

"Having a baby is like meeting a beautiful stranger. You get to fall in love with someone new all over again."

I played at parenting that night, tucking my blanket beneath my mother's chin. She struck childlike poses while she slumbered, her knees tucked up to her stomach, her small, still hands weaved together and folded beneath her face. I watched her, learning what she must have

17

known already—that we are sheltered by our children's unbroken sleep. When I turned away, she pushed her stomach against my back, letting the unborn baby pulse against my kidneys.

I awoke before dawn to the sound of my mother nailing my window sashes to the sills.

"What are you doing?" I asked.

"I'm childproofing," she said. The extra nails bobbed between her lips.

In her last trimester, she had developed a fear of falling. While most expectant women knitted sweaters or cut formula coupons, my mother studied casements and dormers on the second floor of our house. She estimated how far each opened and what part of a child could slip through, continually darting across rooms to shut windows cracked innocently. At breakfast the week before, she'd cited a newspaper story about a toddler who fell from a two-story window into a holly bush and walked away from it with only a few small abrasions. She suggested that my father plant shrubs around the base of our house.

"Which type of bush would have more cushioning power if a baby were to fall into it?" she asked. "A boxwood or a red currant?"

"The red currant," I said, thinking of all the jelly she could make. My father had lifted the newspaper gently from her hands, an amused and troubled look on his face.

Our house was topsy turvy. It had been a four room bungalow with polished oak window seats, coal-burning fireplaces and ten-foot ceilings. The last owner, a man with a big family, had loved the four rooms so much that he'd simply raised the first floor and constructed a second, roomier floor beneath it. Upstairs, the master bedroom and my room were separated by a utilities space with washer and dryer hookup, and as a small child, I could fall asleep only to the sounds of wash and rinse cycles. My mother's bedroom presented the most dangers. A former parlor, its French doors opened out onto a twenty-foot drop down to a brick patio crawling with wild muscadine. She said she hadn't worried about the doors when I was small. With me, her fear had been the swallowing of

18

toxic substances.

"I'll bet you remember what everything in this room tastes like, Anna," she said. "When you were a baby, you tried to eat everything—crumbled plaster, toilet paper, the hearth."

I did remember the perfumey flavor of toilet paper, the iron taste of fireplace brick, each a forbidden pleasure for a curious infant. Before I could tell her this, Mr. Gunn called to finish up a conversation from the night before, and she ran for the phone extension in her bedroom.

"You're not a monster," I heard her say. "If you were such a sick, terrible person, you would have no interest in seeing your children again."

I watched her from the doorway as she cradled the phone between her chin and shoulder, dotting the window casements with a tube of Superglue. The French doors had been locked since we'd moved in and my parents didn't own a key to them. She filled the keyholes with glue. When my father came out of the bathroom, smelling of Old Spice with a towel wrapped around his waist, she hung up the phone and slipped the tube into her pocket.

"Who was that on the phone?" he asked.

"It was Marty Gunn," she said. "Who else would it be?"

My mother laughed breathlessly, but my father's shoulders remained rigid. After he went down to fix breakfast, she pulled up on the window sash, testing the strength of the Superglue. When I stepped into the room, she turned around, surprised and guilty.

"Please don't tell," she said, grabbing my hand.

Who could I tell? I thought. What would I say? That my mother's most recent attempt at motherhood had been Supergluing a window?

"I won't," I said.

"It'll be our little secret."

She put the empty tube back in its package and asked me to throw it out in the garbage can behind the house. On the front of the package, there was a picture of a man who had glued his hard hat to a construction beam. He hung onto his hat, his legs dangling in midair.

Perhaps out of loneliness or nostalgia, Mary's mother allowed Mr. Gunn to come home Sunday afternoon, and she invited our family to join them for dinner. She had Mary call with the invitation, as though the divorce had made her shy with my parents. Mary paused dramatically before speaking into the phone, and my mother hung up on her the first time she called, mistaking her for an obscene caller.

"Mother wants you all to come over for dinner," Mary said when I picked up the phone again.

"What time?"

"Now," she whispered. "As soon as you can get here."

Late afternoon, Mary answered the door with her mother, a quietly pretty woman whose hair had grayed prematurely. Though she had more children, her house was much smaller than ours, and she'd painted the walls in earthtones, beige and sandstone pink. Only the windows were draped with bright floral fabric. My father claimed that Mrs. Gunn could sentence a man to hang by the neck with her soft Georgia accent, and he would enjoy it. She unnerved my mother with her calm, well-considered ways.

"The boys are out bowling tonight," she said when she answered the door. "Anna, Mary Margaret. Go wash your hands and come help us in the kitchen."

While our fathers drank Blue Nun and charred hamburgers on the patio grill, Mrs. Gunn cleaned and boiled shrimp, laying them out in bowls of ice on the kitchen sink. My mother cut thick slices of French bread and poured generous glasses of burgundy for all the adults. Mary and I spread a clean, linen cloth over the dining room table, placing only napkins and plates at each setting. Mrs. Gunn always served simple foods that could be torn and eaten with our hands.

While Mary and I set the table, we listened to our mothers talk quietly in the kitchen.

"Just because I'm not kicking and yelling doesn't mean that I won't go through with it," Mrs. Gunn said.

"I know," my mother said.

"I never thought I'd be a divorced woman," Mrs. Gunn said. "I may as well be wearing a big, scarlet D on my chest."

"The church has changed since Vatican II," my mother said. "It's not as big of a sin."

"I apologize if this dinner makes either of you uncomfortable."

"We cherish the both of you," my mother said. "We wouldn't have it any other way."

"I've got to keep things as stable as possible, for the children. This dinner allows me to do that."

"Of course," my mother said. "Anything you need."

Mary and I were allowed to sit cross-legged on the living room floor and eat windmill cookies for appetizers. By the time dinner was served, we'd guzzled so many bottles of Coke that we had to unzip our jeans and lie down on the floor to relieve our swelling stomachs.

"There is no such thing as heaven," Mr. Gunn said, topping off my parents' wineglasses at the dining room table.

"Where do you think we'll all go then?" my father said.

"I've had a lot of time for reading and reflection lately," Mr. Gunn said, glancing at his wife. "I think we'll all move on to a parallel universe."

"You're an egghead," my father said, laughing.

"I'm sorry." Mr. Gunn wiped his mouth, stood and placed his napkin on his chair. "I'm really sorry." He pushed his chair back abruptly and joined Mary and me in the living room. Lying down on the hardwoods behind the couch, he took off his wire-rimmed glasses and closed his eyes. He was so still that we passed our hands over his mouth to see if he was breathing. Then we backed away from him, embarrassed by his naked grief.

"What's going on?" my mother whispered.

"He feels unworthy of having an opinion," Mrs. Gunn said flatly. She glanced towards us. "Girls, there are cookie crumbs on the floor. Please use your napkins to wipe them up."

After my parents and Mrs. Gunn cleared the table, Mr. Gunn sat up and let us help him build a fire in the fireplace. It was too late in the spring for a fire, but its warmth cheered us. He set his wineglass on the mantel and put *Aida* on the record player.

"I love this aria." He closed his eyes for a moment, and I was afraid he might lie down on the floor again. "Girls, this is the 'Celeste Aida.' It's the part where the captain and Aida cling to each other beneath the Temple of Vulcan. Aida consoles him with her vision of paradise where love will be pure. 'Morir! si pura e bella—Vedi?' Above them, his spurned lover orders them both to be buried alive."

After she cleared the dishes, Mrs. Gunn settled in the love seat and my parents on the couch before the fire. Mr. Gunn wanted to talk about being newlyweds.

"Do you remember when we lived in Tennessee, Barbie?" Mr. Gunn said. "We couldn't afford much of a house, so we looked in the classified ads, where people sell used wedding dresses. We found an ad that read 'Roll up your sleeves. This charming house with land needs some TLC.' We drove up the side of a cliff and along so many winding dirt roads I don't even know how we found the place. It was a barn with holes in the roof. We would have been entombed during the first winter snow. Don't you remember, Barb?"

Mrs. Gunn remained quiet, which only seemed to encourage him. She folded her hands politely in her lap, pulling her feet up beneath her while he talked and paced, throwing his cigarette butts into the fireplace. She was a full head taller than Mr. Gunn, and I wondered how she had ever slowed him down long enough to kiss him.

"We found wild blackberries on the way back down. We stopped the truck to pick them. You carried them in your skirt."

"I had to can blackberry preserves for two days straight," Mrs. Gunn said. "It was hot in that little apartment kitchen. I remember that."

"The gas heater kicked on whenever we used the little air conditioner in the window," he continued, as though this too were a fond memory. "Do you remember when you were pregnant with our first? You were as big as a planet. You'd just gotten out of the bath, and you were too hot to put on clothes to walk past the open window. There were construction workers on the neighbor's roof across the street. When you glanced up and saw them looking in, you just smiled, gave them a little wave and walked on into the bedroom."

"At that point, it just didn't matter anymore," Mrs. Gunn said.

That night, Mr. Gunn recalled every birthday party celebrated, every family vacation taken. Arms folded across her chest, Mrs. Gunn lifted her dry melancholy eyes towards her husband and listened patiently, as though his hopeful memories were something to be waited out, and withstood. When Mr. Gunn said, "There are home movies!" and moved towards the attic stairs, my father stretched his long legs and cracked his toes.

"Well, I've got to get these two and a half people to bed," he said.

Too old to be carried to the car, I faked exhaustion so my father would lift me into his arms, my bare feet bouncing against his calves. He dropped me gently on the front seat, and I rested my head on what was left of my mother's lap, pretending to be asleep. Though it was only a short drive to our house on the next street, my father slipped his shoes off and curled his toes around the gas pedal. The Gunns waved from their front steps. One of their porch lights was burnt out, but the other remained on. As they turned to walk back inside, Mr. Gunn tapped the burnt out bulb and slipped his arm around his wife's waist.

"If we hadn't known about the divorce, do you think tonight would have been different from any other Sunday we've spent at their house?" my father said, his voice hoarse and tired. "It makes me wonder how long they must have lived like that, with all those secrets."

My mother began crying softly.

"What's wrong now?" My father got angry when my mother cried; her sadness was the only thing that made him helpless. "Are we okay?"

After school the next day, Mr. Gunn took Mary and me to his new apartment. For his painting business, he drove a gutted-out ambulance filled with stepladders and half-empty paint cans. We sat next to him on the front seat, shoulder to shoulder, and he let us turn on the siren as we drove a block to an old parsonage broken down into three studios. Outside on the curb, he gave each of us two new brushes and four cans of acrylics so that we could repaint the walls of his apartment.

"Paint whatever you like, girls," he said. "Give me something to remember you by."

We carried the cans and brushes up the wooden stairs that led to his front door. His apartment was the size of a hotel efficiency, dark as a cave, with a bathroom, a living room and small kitchen. He'd pushed a single mattress up against the living room wall, stacking his books—a Bible, a family photo album and *The World History of Art*—against the other. Charcoal sketches were strewn everywhere, flat and crumpled up, spilling over his wastebasket. His refrigerator had broken, so he kept a Styrofoam cooler filled with iced beer, raw oysters, jars of baby corn and calamata olives beside the door. Though my mother served these finger foods at parties, she had sternly warned me, "Don't eat anything while you are at Mr. Gunn's apartment. It could be dangerous."

Mary couldn't wait to show me the bathroom, which was so small the landlord had to stick a glass bubble in the shower ceiling.

"You have to duck into the stall and bathe with your head sticking up in the bubble, like an astronaut." She sounded pleased as she lifted two lead weights from the corners of the tub. "My dad's old scuba weights. He uses them to hold back the shower curtain."

We decided to paint starfish, whales and seahorses on the walls of the bathroom; we drew picture windows on the window-less living room walls and angels on the ceiling. Mr. Gunn slipped his flannel robe over his T-shirt and khaki work pants. While we painted, he paced with his cane behind the kitchen counter, taking sips of Old Crow from his coffee cup, his fingers shaking whenever he lit a new cigarette. He garnished glasses of 7 Up and grenadine with maraschino cherries and gave them to us. On the gas oven range, he perfected a new marinara recipe he called "Lady of the Evening Sauce" that required him to slice up a jar of anchovies. When he opened the front door to air the place out, the cooking smells drew in a black cat with a torn ear, a three-legged mastiff and Desiree, a stripper who lived downstairs and sometimes modeled for him.

Like my mother, Mr. Gunn adopted people who seemed less fortunate than he. Throughout the late afternoon, he listened to fifties radio stations and counseled Desiree. A small blonde who wore beaded moccasins and smoked a dainty pipe, she didn't look very glamorous or pretty, and I said so to Mary.

"Do you think it really matters what her face looks like?" Mary said as we huddled in the shower stall with our paint.

"I'm thinking of taking on a second line of work to bring in more money," Desiree said to Mr. Gunn. "I thought maybe you could help me."

"Oh, really." Mr. Gunn leaned closer to her. "I'm listening."

"I want to be the person who paints street addresses on the curbs in front of houses," she said. "How much do you think I can make?" Mr. Gunn leaned back in his seat.

"Twenty bucks a day," he said. "Now why would a beautiful girl like you want to waste your time on that when you can make hundreds of dollars a night dancing?"

"I can't stand the thought of houses without numbers on them. It's as though the people inside don't exist."

While Mary finished the bathroom, I washed out my paint brushes in the kitchen sink, watching the colors splatter around the drain and onto the kitchen towel. After he walked Desiree to the door, Mr. Gunn stood next to me, replenishing his bourbon. His fingers no longer shook, and he moved in slow motion as he lifted his glass, cocking his head at the running water.

"Ah, the sound of connubial bliss," he said. "Don't turn it off."

Patsy Cline came on the radio.

"Come on, Sugar. Let's dance."

He was only a few inches taller than me, surprisingly graceful for a man with a limp. He twirled us around the room singing, "Crazy. Crazy for feeling so lonely." He stumbled, leaning too close, and I had to support him. I wasn't afraid, but I hadn't thought my first kiss would be like this. His mouth felt smaller than mine, and his hips pressed sharply against me. The taste of whiskey and smoke barely camouflaged the garlic on his breath. As I looked into his handsome, ruined face, I thought, So, this is it? Then he held me back, running a finger over my collar bone,

25

gently cupping my chin in his hands.

"My dear, you have a face that belongs on a Roman coin, like your mother. God forgive me for what I've done." He shook his head. "From now on I am a celibate."

What I saw next was not Desiree or any other dancer. In the darkest corner of the room, I glimpsed shapes so lovely and familiar that I stopped swaying with Mr. Gunn and lifted his hands away. Crammed against the wall were charcoal sketches of a woman, her body bare except for a strand of pearls around her neck. In one pose, she arched her hands above her head like a ballerina; in another, she sat, legs crossed at the ankles, her empty arms outstretched in front of her. There were varicose veins in the creases behind her knees and a pouch of flesh beneath her navel. The left breast sagged lower than the right, a dark mole hidden beneath it. I knew this woman, and I didn't. I felt betrayed by her sad stillness.

"I drew her. Nothing more," Mr. Gunn explained quickly, half-heartedly. "There is nothing wrong with drawing the body."

Mary stepped into the kitchen and turned off the faucet.

"We've got school tomorrow," she said, pulling me out the door and into the evening sunlight.

"Stay a while longer," Mr. Gunn called after us. "Do you really have to leave?" He didn't follow us out the door.

"You knew about it," I said to Mary as we walked down the rickety wooden stairs.

"Wake up," she said, but her voice had lost its jaded quality. "It's what grown ups do."

"Be quiet," I said. "You don't know everything."

Mary and I fled her father's place, running across the grass commons in front of our school to the bakery for a bag of tea cookies. We stuffed ourselves systematically, wordlessly, the sweetness melting across our tongues as we walked home. After we parted at the street corner, I lingered in front of my house, watching my mother work in the flower bed. That false spring, a warm front had fooled our daffodils into blooming in late February, pushing up hard lids of soil. My mother bent

26

the dead flower stems to the ground, lashing them in the middle with a single stem, while I sat on the curb, tossing pebbles into the street. Afraid of confronting her, I felt devoured by adult disappointment.

"Anna, sweetie," she said. "What happened?"

I wanted to curse her, but I hadn't stockpiled the right arsenal of words yet. I wanted to curl up in her lap, letting her French braid my hair.

What I said was, "Will you please tell me what it means to be womanly?" She stood, massaged her stiff back and walked slowly towards me, as though this were her answer. *You might fall in love more than once and dance on tables. You might glue all the windows of your house shut. You will learn to close doors and bury secrets.* Her eyes were tired, but she seemed as full and round as any planet, waiting for the new life inside her to begin.

Player Piano

After a day of printing invitations,
after a night class spent deciphering
the calculus of angle and line
he carried home popcorn kernels
that slid like pearls through his wife's fingers
into spitting oil, trembling, splitting, blossoming.
She poured salt, ladled popcorn like soup
into her mother's good china tureen,
served it in china bowls with good silver spoons.
He took off his shoes, shuffled to the player piano,
opening its case to inspect the parts he'd reassembled.
His hands too ink-stained to touch the ivory,
he clung to the handle beneath the keys,
pedaling, turning the wheels
pulling paper rolls over the gold organ
that breathed music through holes,
Oh Promise Me, Rhapsody in Blue, Sweet Gypsy Rose.
He sweated, swaying beside her narrow back,
her still hands caught against her flat stomach.
She leaned into him, flipped
the switch to change the key, turning
the piano's rich wood tunes hollow.
Beneath the melody the paper music crackled,
pedals thumped against the case,
the bench creaked and rocked beneath their weight,
the room spinning with Ragtime Jazz, Canadian Sunset,
Amazing Grace.

My Mother's War Stories

When I was thirteen, my father lost his job and devoted his life to Civil War re-enactment. Two nights before Labor Day, I polished the infantry shoes he would wear as he led his rebel troop against the Army of the Ohio at a primitive re-enactment festival. My parents' voices rose then fell as low as the hum of my mother's sewing machine behind the closed door of the attic workroom. My mother had called my father's romance with war foolishness, the root of our financial worries; it was the pretense for most of their arguments. As their fighting began, it felt like all our lives were as stillborn as the children who came before me.

"I pulled hundreds of homeless Cubans from the Gulf of Mexico," my father said. "I know what a crisis is. We're not having one."

My mother told him to stop talking like a war veteran.

"The closest you've ever come to real action was when we conceived Anna," she said.

My father swore that if she took the bus back to her mother's house in Charleston she could stay there forever, but she would leave me, his only living daughter, in Ohio with him. Then he stormed out of the workroom. Down in the kitchen, he heated canned corned beef in a pot of boiling water and invited me to eat supper with him in his study.

"The Union soldiers called this 'embalmed meat,' " he said, scraping the beef off his plate with a corner of toast. As company historian, my father lined his bookshelves with worn copies of the *On the Bloodstained Field* and the *Gray Ghosts of the Confederacy.* He'd covered his study walls with cork and pinned up a print of a Confederate prisoner of war, a gaunt, sad-eyed man with water dripping off the bill of his cap, the words "Soldier in the Rain; His Only Weapon is Hope" beneath the picture. A second generation Italian from Cincinnati, my father was as southern as a gypsy. I never asked him why he always sided with

31

the Confederacy; I assumed he held some romantic fascination with my mother's Charleston roots.

I picked up the knight from my father's Civil War chess set— a solid pewter J.E.B. Stuart mounted on horseback, a tiny feather in his cap.

"You look just like J.E.B. Stuart," I said.

"You think so?" He ran a hand through his thinning hair, glancing shyly into the mirrored squares of the chess board. He shook his head. "Nope. J.E.B. had all his hair. He was as flashy as a prince."

He pulled a striped scarf from his pocket and spun it into a belt. Then he arranged it over his shoulder like a sling.

"This cloth is a medical kit, a cleaning rag and a belt," he said. "If you're wounded in a war, you could dip the end of this in alcohol, put a knot in it and push it into the wound to jerk out the infection. It could also be a necktie."

That night, my father and I lost ourselves in historical facts. For instance, every once in a while you could stand ten feet away from a battle and hear only silence. A fold in the ground or a strong wind could block out all sounds of canons and muskets, causing a silent battle. When my father was a boy, a schoolmate shot an eraser into his left ear. The doctor broke his eardrum when he tried to remove it, and now my father held a silent battle every day as he strained to hear conversations to his left.

"I think she's getting worse," I said into his bad ear, half-hoping he wouldn't hear me. "Maybe we should take her to a doctor."

"Your mother doesn't need a doctor," he said. "Her problem is that she wants every day to be a birthday party, preferably her own."

"Do you think she's going to leave us?" I said.

I heard rustling behind my mother's workroom door.

"Go check on her, will you?" He bowed his head over his Civil War field manual, and that's when my mother threw her sewing machine out the window.

The gears of the machine had quickened, clanking like a derailed train, then stopped. A window in her room slid open. A black heap fell past my own window into a bed of geraniums that lined the front porch.

Afraid that she'd thrown herself out the window, my father and I ran to her room. She lay on her side, her face against the wall where the slanted ceiling met the floor. Her wild copper hair flamed across her gray shawl. My father sat next to her, tall and broad-shouldered as J.E.B. Stuart, folded his hands in his lap and calmly waited for her to finish weeping. Only his eyes betrayed fear as he stared at the empty sewing table and her shaking back.

"Go back to the study, Anna," he said. "You shouldn't have seen this."

I returned to the study and ironed the skirt I would wear at the re-enactment festival as I recited stories about Clara Barton while my father fought against the Union troups. It seemed as though I'd been excluded from all crucial action that year. First, I'd been demoted from soldier to nurse when I'd discreetly slipped my bra out through the sleeve of my flannel uniform because it slid about as I lifted my breech loader musket. Now, I would have to wait uselessly in the next room as my mother wept. The skirt was gray and ankle-length, and it landed as heavily as an Army blanket when I tossed it across the room. I paced to the doorway and back, then threw myself on the couch, waiting for them to call me back into my mother's room.

Hours later, a bolero rose from my mother's record player, muffling their hushed voices. Her mahogany bed creaked and rocked to the drums as the headboard beat against the wall. My mother sighed while my father cried out hoarsely, brutally, as though the two were engaged in the most ancient of struggles.

The next morning, I brewed some coffee and took it to my mother's room. The wardrobe doors were thrown open. All her cocktail dresses had been torn off padded hangers and wadded between bolts of cloth, while others were draped over her open suitcase on the floor. On the wall above her worktable, my family's Easter palm fronds were braided, dried and tucked behind an oil painting of Christ's last supper. The wedding ring quilt on the spare bed had been turned down neatly from feather pillows in the silk cases my father had brought back from

Japan when he was in the Navy, claiming silk could prevent split ends.

My mother had earned grocery money that year by making bed jackets. An apprentice seamstress and an ex-music and English teacher, she was the only grown woman with eyesight I'd ever known who did not have a driver's license. She took taxis to our church where she sat at card tables in the basement and read *The Odyssey* to the elderly parishioners who bought her sewing. My father had turned fifty that spring. Denied early retirement by the man who'd fired him from selling vending machines, he'd been replaced by three, twenty-one-year old college graduates. A quiet man, my father had been looking forward to retirement since the beginning of his career. He would not move down to Charleston to "start over" as my mother suggested. Instead, he ran his brother's printing press for half his old salary and re-enacted battles in soggy cow pastures just north and south of the Ohio River.

My mother turned from her empty sewing table with the long, gray Clara Barton skirt in her arms.

"Here, try this on," she said. The front sagged below my ankles, but the back rose up dangerously close to my underpants. She pulled it roughly from me, the straight pins scratching my legs. As she ripped out the hem with a hooked thimble, she rambled on about love, her favorite subject.

"I know you do more than hold hands when you are alone with your boyfriend," she said. "I fumbled around in the back seats of quite a few cars with boys before I married your father." She was speaking of Nathan, the boy from the disturbed adolescents shelter across the street. I'd befriended him earlier that summer.

"Nathan is not my boyfriend," I said.

"I see you out under the streetlamp, heads bent towards each other like two lovebirds."

"He's sixteen," I said. "He's been to jail."

She frowned, looked into her slender hands, and I felt guilty for correcting her.

"Your father was a hood when I met him. He wore tight black chinos and rolled his cigarettes up in his T-shirt sleeves. He gave all that up for me and joined the Navy."

Embarrassed for my mother, I was afraid of where this story would lead. She habitually shed our dark family secrets like filthy overcoats, claiming that open people were healthier than those who kept their lives private. My father called her confessions "war stories," but they were really allegories with morals often lost on me.

"I wasn't much older than you when the three babies before you came cold and blue as skim milk, the umbilical cords wrapped around their necks. All day and night, I stayed by myself at a beach house while your father stood watch on a pier in Key West, pulling Cubans out of the water. After the third stillborn, I stopped playing the piano.

"I remember walking down to the pier in the middle of the night to see your father. I was bored and lonely, and I just wanted to talk to him. When he saw me coming, he kept looking into the black water. I asked him why he was helping *them,* and he said, 'Because they're not hurting anyone.' "

I understood the message of this story, but I could not apply it to my own life. I hardly knew Nathan, and I did not intend to have his child. Once, I'd asked my mother why she married my father and she said, "I was very young. He was handsome. He owned a car." Because of her, I equated love with sorrow, and I wondered how their marriage, so complex and disappointing, could have begun with a school girl's simple desires.

She threw the skirt onto the floor and laughed nervously. "Who am I kidding? I'm not a seamstress."

"Little old women love you," I said. "Maybe you could get a job at a nursing home."

"What are we going to do if your father doesn't find a good job?"

"He has work," I said. "We'll be just fine."

I took her hand and led her to the basement where we kept a giant, walnut player piano. In autumn, my father searched flea markets and antique stores for scrolls of music to play on the piano. I pumped the pedals that turned the rolls of paper music while my mother sang "King of the Road" and "I Never Promised You A Rose Garden." When she grew melancholy, she asked for the Mozart sonata that she no longer could play. As she sat on the piano bench beside me, her face pinched from mourning the abandoned skill, I imagined my mother was pretending to be one of my lost sisters. I wondered how I had become a sister to my own mother and why my father seemed unable to offer her much comfort. When I was small, she'd called me "the missing link," a child with her eyes and my father's chin. I understood now that I must bridge the space between her, my father and the rest of the world. I felt inept, but absolutely necessary.

My father had become a printer's devil, an apprentice who cleaned and set type for my uncle, and although it should have been his day off, he took me to work at the printing shop early the next morning. The dark, cramped room was lined with wooden type cases. The air smelled thick with petroleum ink. A black iron cylinder press stood like a medieval torture device in the corner. Beside it were a guillotine used to cut sheaves of paper, and the paddy wagon, a rack with screws used to flatten and glue paper into note pads.

My job was to clean and sort the type while my father put new type in the chase of the letter press and locked it up. I wiped the used letters down with gasoline-soaked rags and tied them together with string. The day before, my father had asked my uncle if he could become a partner in the printing business, and my uncle had said that he couldn't afford to share that much of the profits. My mother had locked herself in her workroom after hearing the news.

"Why won't Uncle Joe make you his partner? He's as rich as a king," I said.

"Your uncle and I grew up in the Over the Rhine projects. He drives all his potential employees down past the cold-water flat he and I grew up in," my father explained. He lifted the heavy type frame and rings of sweat appeared beneath the arms of his white, button-down dress shirt. "He always says the same thing: 'That's where I come from, and I'll do anything so that I don't end up there again.'"

Like my mother, my father rarely answered a question directly. For hours, he arranged words backwards on a tombstone to keep them level. Lead type clicked against granite like the slow ticking of a clock. We kept the overhead lights off to stay cool, but the humid afternoon breeze blew in the open door until my mind became numb with heat and boredom. At five o'clock, my father looked up from his work and stood. As he carried the type to the chase, his sleeve caught on an iron shaft. Letters flew like shrapnel everywhere and our day's work landed on the floor like a broken jigsaw puzzle. My back and feet ached, but I wanted to run into the street, never to return to that sweltering shop. I let out an involuntary cry.

"For Christ sakes, Anna. Why did you scream like that?"

"I'm sorry," I said. "I'm tired."

"Go on home," he said. "Tell your mother that I won't be there for supper."

My father fell to his knees, searching blindly beneath the press in the gritty blackness for the lost letters. His hands were raw from the gasoline, but there was still ink on his palms and beneath his fingernails. It occurred to me that he was a kind, patient man whose hands would never be clean again.

After supper, I sat on the front curb, side-arming gravel into the street, waiting for my father to return. We lived in the historical district of our town, where shabby homes with high ceilings and gingerbread trim could be bought with small down payments. Our neighbors continually repaired their siding and sowed shade grass into the mud beneath their cedar and tulip trees. Throughout spring and summer, ladders remained propped against blaze roses that climbed the sides of houses. After my father lost his job and my mother became more reclusive, the neighbors avoided our house the way they avoided the county home for disturbed adolescents, the yellow colonial across the street. At dusk, while the other neighbors gossiped over hedges about lead paint disclosures and termites, my father often joined Mrs. Hoffman, the house mother from the shelter, to swap home remedies—whole garlic cloves to cure the common cold, honey and vinegar to strengthen a weak heart.

In the front lawn of the shelter, a family had planted a Christmas evergreen years before. It had overtaken most of the lawn, its branches tapping against the second-floor windows of the house. Through the branches, I saw a girl nearing the eighth month of pregnancy, her frame so tiny that she could wear unzipped men's blue jeans instead of the donated maternity clothes. She passed in front of the window, screaming at Mrs. Hoffman, "I think you are the devil." Whenever I missed curfew, my father said that I would end up pregnant in that house.

Nathan slammed the front screen door and marched across the street.

"Hey, Scout," I said.

"Don't call me that," he said.

"Why?" I said. "Aren't you always prepared?"

He sat down next to me and twisted the lid off a bottle of Old Crow. A doe-eyed boy who'd failed all high school subjects except history, Nathan often drank too much and told me he'd mourned the death of John Lennon more than the death of his own father. As we passed his bottle to each other, a curtain moved in my mother's attic window, and the glass rose stealthily. The bass drums of a bolero floated out the window and down to the driveway.

"What's that?" Nathan said.

"It's a love song," I said. "My mother thinks you're my boyfriend."

"Your mother's cool."

"She's crazy," I said.

I jumped up, leaned against my family's green Toronado, but Nathan stood too, pinning me against the hood. His sharp tongue darted in my mouth, burning like the bourbon at the back of my throat. The primal drum beat floated out my mother's window and made my arms and legs weak with longing. Night air seeped through my open zipper as his cool fingers felt beneath my underwear. I wanted him to keep touching me, but his eyes were filled with sadness and rage, and I pulled away from him.

"I can't," I said. "I'm Italian and Catholic. My mother says I'm extremely fertile."

Cramped, nauseous from his deep kisses, I felt sorry for him. He

38

stumbled from the car and tipped the rest of the bourbon into his mouth. After flinging the bottle into the hens and chickens plants, he staggered to the rear fender and began lifting the car—a technique his own father had once said would combat sexual frustration. Dropping the car, then lifting, he let it bounce on the pavement. Then he ran out into the street.

"When my old man was in the army, he fell asleep while he was supposed to be on night watch. When he woke up the next day, the Viet Cong had paid a visit. He found his whole troop sitting cross legged, leaning against a fence, holding their heads in their laps."

"Stop it," I said. "You're scaring me."

"I don't think he was crazy though, not like your mother." He turned abruptly, walked behind the evergreen and slammed the screen door behind him.

"She's not really crazy." My words flew against the locked door of the shelter and floated into the night air. I walked back to my house. Repulsed by his terrible story, I wondered why he'd told it to me so soon after we'd kissed. Perhaps there was no one else he could tell. My mother's shattered sewing machine lay on the grass beneath the red currant bush, like the possum that crawled up and died there at the height of dry summer. I regretted not giving it a proper soldier's burial.

The next morning, my father asked me to keep an eye on my mother while he went early to the battle field. He told me to escort her to church and then to meet him at the festival behind Saint Rita's School for the Deaf at noon. After he left, my mother appeared at my bedroom door, dressed in a peasant blouse and skirt, swinging a pair of spiked, leather sandals at her side.

"I'm ready," she said, then went downstairs to wait while I showered and dressed.

As we waited for our taxi to Our Lady of the Rosary church, I told her that Nathan and I had fought.

"Go talk to him," she said. "Maybe you can still get him back."

"I don't think I had him to begin with," I said.

My mother's interest in my love life depressed me, and I shifted uneasily from one foot to another.

"It breaks my heart to see you so unhappy," she said.

"I'm not unhappy."

"My father walked out on my mother when I was your age," she said. "He just left all his clothes hanging in his closet, like he'd died. I read the note he left for her. It said, 'I'm going off to look for love.' He married a woman who squandered our family's fortune. He died alone, impoverished, too embarrassed to go back to my mother."

Again, I tried to interpret my mother's story and apply it to my own life, but Nathan and I weren't married and there wasn't any money left to lose.

Inside the taxi, my mother discussed job possibilities.

"Don't tell your father, but I'm going back to school," she said. "I'm going to be a travel agent."

"I'll be your first customer." I was still brooding from the night before. "You can send me to Alaska."

At the church door, we dipped our fingers in the font, touching the dissolving sponge and crossing ourselves with tepid holy water. Although it was a drafty old church with stone floors, new aluminum air conditioning pipes and ducts had been built above the stained glass windows. It appeared as though the church were on life support. At the altar, we placed quarters in the wrought-iron box and lit a red votive candle, then lowered ourselves onto cracked leather kneelers.

For as long as I could remember, my mother had waged a war against God through a young priest named Father Edward. He cut an angelic figure with straight, white teeth and a blond, curly beard. He wore ripped blue jeans and cowboy boots beneath his robes, and my mother once had an unholy crush on him. After I was born, she'd confessed taking the pill because she could not bear another stillbirth; he'd told her that she'd never be a good Catholic.

She hadn't spoken to the priest since then. When I grew old enough, she urged me into the confessional once a month because, by God, she'd save her daughter's soul if she could not save her own. Looking down into my hands, I'd invented sins when I ran out of real ones: "Father, I stole wine from the sacristy," or, "Father, I told Sister Agnes that I'd chosen Mary Magdalene for my confirmation name just so that she would cry." Every month, I'd gone obediently behind the heavy purple curtain, enduring the silent scorn of the priest because this seemed so important to my mother, but the morning after the bolero catastrophe, I turned on her.

"I'm not going to confession anymore," I said. "If you've got something to say to Father Edward, you need to say it yourself."

She drew her breath, backed away from me as though I'd slapped her, but she stood up. As she disappeared into the tiny curtained room, I moved into the last pew and waited. She came out too quickly, followed by an old cleaning lady who must have been dusting the empty confessional. There was a dazed look of wonderment on my mother's face, as though she'd seen a vision.

"Father Edward ran off with a nun to live in Hawaii." She looked toward the cry room, where mother's held children on Sunday mornings and priests held memorials on Friday nights. I realized then that she'd put all her trust in a lying priest instead of a daydreaming soldier.

Afraid of leaving her alone, I took my mother with me to meet my father at the festival. Saint Rita's School for the Deaf looked like an abandoned stone mansion on a hill overlooking the interstate. I'd ridden past the school hundreds of times, but I had never seen the deaf children playing outside. Now, I imagined them watching the festival from inside the darkened windows like small, quiet ghosts.

In the field below the school, we entered a circle of tents. A light rain fell, soaking the paper snow cone cups that littered the field. The air smelled of rain and gun powder. I ducked into David "Spirit Bear" Hildebrand's bead working tent.

"Hey, it's the angel of the battlefield," he said. "Is your daddy gonna bleed those Yankees white today?"

"I hope so," I said.

Under the next tent, the chaplain for the police and fire department played a dulcimer, reading from the Book of Daniel for those who'd stop to listen. In the center of the encampment, my father's troop performed the manual of arms. Some of the men rested rifles against their shoulders; others aimed in front of them. They marched out to the center of the field and fired blanks at the Ole Caintuckee Primitives, then broke up laughing as the men and women in buckskin jumped and cursed.

I found a lawn chair for my mother, settled a blanket over her lap and watched my father reorganize his troop, a group of men aged thirteen to sixty-five, dressed in gaudy, mismatched brown or gray flannel shirts. He walked a step ahead of them, his thinning hair rippling in the slight breeze.

For dramatic effect, I always twisted the bottom of my skirt with my hands as I told the story of Clara Barton.

"Clara Barton worked next to doctors who stacked amputated limbs on the ground, legs in one pile, arms in another," I began. "The hem of her skirt would become so bloody that she had to wring it out before she could run onto the battlefield to nurse the soldiers."

"When the soldier next to you falls, move to the right and fill in the ranks," my father yelled. "Forward."

As his troop ran to the front line, my father dropped his knapsack, his bowie knife, anything that would weigh him down as he charged the Union front. He ran into sulphuric blue smoke, a graceless angel running through clouds. After a sharp crackle of muskets, he crawled over the bodies of fallen men. The minister's words, "Whoever does not fall down to worship this image shall be thrown in a burning furnace," rose above canon and gun shot, and for a moment I believed I was in the midst of a silent battle. Then, like actors deserting a script, my father's troop and his enemies stopped fighting and quietly turned towards him. He was facing my mother who now stood in the middle of the field, her spiked heels sinking into the mud, her hands on her hips.

"Why do you always have to be on the losing side?" she said.

"The Union needs someone to battle," he said. "Now will you please sit down, Rose Marie."

"I don't believe you," she said. "You'd rather be a dying soldier than talk to me. You do this for spite."

"We'll discuss this at home. You could have gotten hurt out here. Someone could have knocked you down or worse."

"War is hell, isn't it." My mother turned and staggered off the muddy field, her long hair whipping against her face. As she disappeared into a stand of pines at the far edge of the field, I thought of chasing her, but I turned to my father first.

"Should I go get her?" I said.

"Let her go."

Sitting on a patch of wild onions, mud drying on his hands and face, he no longer looked heroic. Whatever spirit had moved him towards near victory on the battlefield had escaped like a single, deep breath. His shoulders sagged. His face was worn and haggard, tormented by all the adult secrets he'd tried to keep from me.

Nathan sat on the curb of our driveway, waving my father's car down as we approached.

"Your mother's at the shelter," he reported as we parked the car. "She's been there for an hour. She asked me to take her back. What did she mean by that?"

Inside, the shelter's family room looked like an archeologist's dig. The house mother's biological son returned once a month to scatter trilobites, brachiopods and ancient bird fossils across end tables and the hearth. My mother sat cross-legged on the floor in front of the TV, her hair hanging over her face like a veil. Her bare feet were raw with blisters from walking five miles in ill-fitting shoes. She laughed strangely while the evening newscaster announced a car bombing in a disinterested voice. Nathan stood against the wall, his face solemn and anxious. The pregnant girl I'd seen the night before sat on the couch, shooting curious scornful glances at my mother's back.

I turned to watch Mrs. Hoffman. In a month, my mother would run away to live with her own mother in Charleston, and my father would not bring her back home. Mrs. Hoffman would wrap my father's Confederate uniform in tissue paper and pack it into a box of his field manuals marked for Good Will. Then she would take him to her own bed. But now, this plain solid woman put her arm around my mother's shoulders, a gesture she reserved for her foster children.

"She wasn't hurting anyone, so I let her stay," she said.

"Rosie," my father said. "It's me. It's Anna too. We need you at the home front."

"I talked to him," my mother said, laughing girlishly, her eyes too wide. "It's settled. He'll take us back." She looked beyond my face, never focusing on anything. As my father moved towards her, she dodged him as though one firm embrace would splinter her frail body.

My father lifted my mother in his arms firmly, gently, and she collapsed against his chest. As he carried her across the street to our house, I watched the crease in the back of his knees, waiting for his thin legs to buckle. In the bathroom, when he lowered her feet into a tub of Epsom salts, I watched from the doorway, imagining him pulling half-drowned women and children from the Gulf of Mexico. His face and shoulders silhouetted against midday sunlight, he must have looked like the shadow of a god reaching down from heaven. He wrapped my mother's feet in a rough green towel, telling her stories from his childhood.

"When I was Anna's age, I took a job delivering fruit downtown," he said. "I'd lied about my age, so I had to teach myself how to drive. You should have seen me grinding the gears, the grapefruit truck lurching up and down the alleys."

As I listened, I could not distinguish between real events and my father's mythology. Later, I learned that this did not matter. My father told those stories to stop time, postponing the moment when he must decide my mother's fate. Earlier that summer, our neighbors had gossiped on driveways while their children caught fire flies, writing their names with the green, fluorescent bodies on the sidewalk while above them, cicadas buzzed like a looming airplane. The night my father carried my mother away from the disturbed adolescent's shelter and over the threshold of our home, the fall air seemed deadly quiet, as though parents, children and insects had settled down to an uneasy truce.

Tarantata

The dark hours—
scrambled eggs, tap water
beyond the kitchen window
crepe myrtle twists like skinned muscle
into scrub oak and holly. Fallen summer leaves
no longer shield me
from black and broken windows
in the home for unwed mothers
behind my house.
One of the girls has left
a bureau sinking into mud, teenage lingerie
foaming from its top drawer.
I am reminded of Italian daughters
bitten by the spider
of unnamed desires, tarantatas fleeing
through orchards, falling
into spinning dance for three days, collapsing
in church ruins,
heads rolling, white peasant skirts tangled
between bare legs, waiting
for the men to offer
violins, tambourines, voices:
Figliola, mother, virgin, fountain
climb the mountain, enter
the garden, go across waters, make
this young girl happy, heal her.
The moon is white and you are dark

In a letter from a former student
on God's mission in a rainforest,
she writes of wind and rain, the call
of monkeys, bright birds at night.
The rains are so soft
but they come every day. Mold
grows on my walls and ceiling, clinging
between creases in my skirts.
I am not lonely.
A school girl brought me her tarantula.
She was very natural with holding
and letting it crawl all over her.
Some tarantulas are poisonous.
This one hardly bites
and his venom is weak.
These words conjure her dark eyes,
stories of her mother who gave up painting for children,
drank coffee inside a child's empty teepee.
When do girls stop believing in spun myths
of women happy to be still?
In the backyard's late-winter ruin,
sharp holly leaves prick
my bare feet. Moonlight softens
the home for unwed mothers. Mold
clambers down its slate roof
like black and harmless spiders.

Pilgrimage to the Black Madonna

In my letters home from Poland, I called Beata my traveling companion, my student, my close acquaintance, but I never called her my lover. She was married to an unemployed history teacher who drank vodka from foggy cough syrup bottles and sang Jesus songs all morning. Every Tuesday and Thursday afternoon, while she served her husband brown bread with potatoes and then watched him fall asleep on the torn leather couch beside their kitchen table, I waited impatiently for her to knock on my door with a bottle of Bulgarian red wine under one arm and a crumpled bag of ginger cookies from Torun clenched in her fist.

"Christopher," she'd say, holding the wine bottle to my lips. "You and I will send this baby to Jesus. Okay?"

She'd line her shoes up under my bed and slide under the coarse wool blanket with me, naked, massaging my abdomen, then lower, and we'd make love until dusk, stopping only to eat and drink an entire day's pay from the teacher's training college where she ran the library and I taught English to young Polish women.

But one early September afternoon, as I waited in bed for Beata, I heard shuffling in the rectory hallway and unlocked the door for two grandmothers who were touching the crucifix on the pale green wall and pouring holy water from the font into a ceramic crock. Their shoulders were hunched like those of gargoyles; they'd tied rags around their swollen ankles to walk into town.

"When will you lead pilgrimage to Czestochowa to see the black Madonna?" the shorter woman said.

"I'm not a priest," I said. "You must speak to Father Tadeusz."

She shook her hennaed hair and laughed. "You speak like a child. Tell me when we will go."

She'd never heard an American speak Polish, and I knew that she would refuse to understand me. I began shaking my head and pointing to the floor, towards the pastor's apartment. She laughed and said something about wanting to make a confession. I took the women to Father Tadeusz's door and knocked. He wasn't home, so I gave up and accepted their gifts of cabbage rolls and pierogi. I agreed to lead them to the black Madonna the following night so that they would go away. The second old woman urged me to blow the sign of the cross over her crock of holy water, my breath the spirit that would leave her twice blessed, and then she closed my door.

The only native English speaker in Biala Podlaska, a town that bordered White Russia, I'd been teaching classes called "Education for Democracy" since the wall fell. Housing was short, so in return for my services, the college boarded me in the town's rectory. The day I moved in, the school's director and Beata came to my rooms. They gave me a fork, a spoon, a knife and a bowl for my tiny, empty kitchen. Beata said she knew how to find stock pots, spatulas, any kitchen appliance I needed at the Russian flea market. The next day, Beata returned alone with an electric kettle. She said she'd never met an American man, but that she'd seen *The Love Connection* on the British Sky cable channel; she knew that in America men liked to cook for themselves. She said she wondered what it would feel like to sleep with an American man. Intrigued, I offered to show her, but after the first time, I began to want her near me. I grew used to her warm smell of cooking grease and exhaust; I needed to hear her soft voice whispering in English when the jagged sounds of Polish spoken on the streets and in the halls of the rectory isolated and overwhelmed me.

For two years, I lectured on the Puritans, Thoreau, the Emancipation Proclamation, and during this time, I'd seen Paderewski's remains blessed and buried beneath liberated soil and crucifixes hung on all the college's classroom walls. My students had begun telling me they wanted only English lessons from me, that they wanted out of Poland and they needed only spoken English skills to leave. We met at bars, instead of in the classroom, and the students felt most comfortable around me when I propped my feet on the table and slugged down Okociem beer, saying in my American oil-tycoon voice, "This here's a cute little bar. I

48

think I'll buy it."

I heard another knock on my door, and the rectory's housekeeper bustled in, ready to beat my bed clothes with a wire hanger. I watched Pani Agnieszka's rounded shoulders as she folded the red wool blanket over the iron rail of my apartment's back porch and began slapping at it, casting hair and body ash like evil spirits into the gritty September wind. When she finished, she placed the blanket at the foot of the bed, nodded as I gave her a German chocolate bar, and then scurried back to the basement. There, I knew she would sit on a metal cot in a cement cell with her hands folded, eyeing a slender crucifix on the cold gray wall until she was ordered to serve cabbage and kielbasa at that evening's *kolacja*.

I went back to bed. I planned to tell Father Tadeusz about the pilgrimage later, but for now, as on most afternoons here, I wanted to sleep. I stared at the cracked walls of my immense apartment, barren except for a red curtained window and a short wave radio on the Formica kitchen table. I thought of Beata covering her mouth with her hand, her face crimson as the school's director said she could not attend classes because her English was too shabby. When we were alone in my apartment, Beata spoke English better than any of my students. Her head bowed shyly, strands of hair falling over her round green eyes and blemished face, she read Whitman aloud to me. *Whoever you are, now I place my hand upon you, that you be my poem, I whisper with my lips close to your ear, I have loved many women and men, but I love none better than you.* Although the director said that a country that produced *Dynasty* and *Dallas* could not be the home of any real writers, Beata wrote to the American embassy to ask for more books. Her library was a damp basement with metal shelves filled with old high school government textbooks and glossy magazines with titles like *Healing With Herbs*, but I found Faulkner and Anderson too when I hid there on gloomy afternoons. Very often now, I was convinced there was no one here worth helping, including myself, and that Beata was the only generous spirit in this town.

I heard a light tap on my door, and I imagined Beata leaning against the wall in the hallway, her hair damp with sweat from running to the rectory.

49

Then I heard Father Tadeusz clear his throat and I opened the door for him. He looked at the rumpled bedclothes.

"You go to bed too early, Christopher," he said. "I must show you my American music. Then we will have, as you Americans say, a brewsky."

I followed him down the dark stairway, then into his large apartment. I surveyed his collection of pirated tapes stacked up the wall, his stereo speakers the size of my small refrigerator. He opened a bottle of vodka.

"A gift from a parishioner," he said. "You like Rolling Stones?"

Until now, I'd felt guilty about my short wave radio, a gift from my students.

"So you have many Polish girlfriends," he said.

"No," I said.

"Ah, but you would like many Polish girlfriends. Napoleon once said that Polish women were the only reason for conquering this country."

"I'm not here to conquer your country."

"Why are you here?"

"I'm not sure," I said. "I thought I knew when I came here, but I don't know anymore."

Pani Agnieszka shuffled into the room carrying two bowls of cabbage with dill and kielbasa. The cherry compote she served was luke warm, and I craved an ice cube. Father Tadeusz ground pepper onto the food and shoveled it into his mouth while his widowed sister waited on him. When he finished, he passed the empty bowl back to her, his face turned sharply away from her face.

"Two grandmothers asked me to lead them to Czestochowa next week," I said in English. "I need you to explain who I am, and that I cannot lead pilgrimages."

He smiled and leaned back in his chair. "I think it would be good for you to lead pilgrimage. They do not need priest for walking. You are my town's American Saint Christopher. They want you more than they want me."

"So you won't tell them?"

50

"It will be a good thing for you to experience. You will go tomorrow night. You will see the black Madonna at dawn. Go thy way in safety." He laughed at himself and tipped his glass back. Back home in Bluefield, when I took my grandmother to the Sacred Heart Church, I'd seen railroad officials more powerful than priests swill back the last of the blessed wine, and while watching Father Tadeusz, I was reminded of these men. Warned that even the Russians went blind from this drink, I sipped carefully, keeping the glass nearly full. My throat burned and a sharp pain began above my left eye. I blocked his hand as he attempted to pour.

"No more," I said, and then I walked out.

I went to the rectory kitchen where Pani Agnieszka was baking onion rolls and scrubbing her brother's socks and clerical collars in a plastic washtub before she threw them into the washing machine. She'd once told me that as a girl, she'd been a dancer in Krakow. Patches of scalp showed through her gray hair, which she crimped and twisted like coils of thin wire against her head. Her swollen ankles were wrapped with rags like the country women. She mixed French with English and a little bit of Polish when she spoke to me. Once, I'd seen her carrying wood for the kitchen's fireplace at the town market. Bent over with branches stacked on her back, she'd looked like a crooked, moving bush.

"Father Tadeusz wants me to lead a group of pilgrims to the black Madonna next week," I said.

"She is not really black, you know," Pani Agnieszka said.

"Have you seen her?" I asked.

"Mais bien sur. Every good Catholic Pole has seen her."

"I'm not a good Catholic."

"But you have a good Catholic name."

"I've heard."

"Saint Christopher carried the child Jesus, as heavy as the sins of the world, across the river," she said.

"And so I should be able to escort two grandmothers to the black Madonna?"

"When I was a girl, I walked barefoot from Krakow to see the

51

black Madonna. Along the way, I stepped on a rusted nail. It was so deep in my foot that it broke off and my mother could not get it out. She soaked my foot in salt water, wrapped it and carried me on her back for two days. When we arrived, she set me down on the skirts of the black Madonna. She unwrapped my foot and cried when she saw the red stripes shooting away from the wound. My toes were black, and my mother cried so hard because she knew I would not walk again. Then she looked up and saw the black Madonna's tears. My mother took the tears, mixed them with her own and bathed my foot. The next day, I walked home without pain."

I rose, grabbed an onion roll which warmed the palms of my hands. She'd turned towards the brick oven. As I pushed the door open, she grabbed my arm and said, "I am telling the truth to you. She is miraculous. If you go there, please come back and tell me how she is. Take some more bread before you go."

Next to the rectory, the new brick church rose like a medieval castle beneath split wood scaffolding. I had never seen the workers, but the church grew taller and new windows had been installed in place of the shattered ones each time I saw it. I moved into the night, along dusty gravel roads and past black-barred kiosks, towards the center of town. I passed the new western grocery market with orange bars on its windows. Inside the glass, a jar of peanut butter and a can of Campbell's soup were displayed on emerald cloth, like jewels. I headed towards the town pub where I hoped Beata would be waiting for me. Beata's grandmother cooked the evening meal when Beata worked late hours at the library and then went out for a drink with me. Beata said she felt sad when she returned after midnight to her dark apartment, but never guilty. She said her grandmother had become a mother to her own husband.

On evenings like this, I felt useless and drained, like everyone here wanted something from me, but no one would tell me what it was. I'd fantasize about sneaking out of the country without saying goodbye to anyone. I'd arrive in my hometown of Bluefield, Virginia, and head straight for the Food Lion to buy a porterhouse, a half gallon of coffee ice cream, and a large tea with ice cubes. Then I imagined my father's voice rolling like his beloved, old mountains, saying, "No one here knows what you've been doing over there, and no one cares. It's like you dropped off the face of the earth. When you are through roaming, what will you do?"

I walked the dark dusty streets, feeling the vodka seep into my arms and legs like fatigue. I thought about saints. I'd learned from my grandmother that Saint Lucy appeared in visions holding the eyes once gouged out of her head in the palms of her hands. Saint Lawrence, grilled over a pit of flames, had said before dying, "Turn me over. I'm done on this side." And I'd learned that the dead rose from their graves to meet St. Thomas as he drove a fiery chariot through churchyards at night. These were my heroes when I was a child, a circle of warm-blooded friends, but now they were ghost stories and I longed for the time when I still believed in them. I stopped once and yelled out. "I am not a goddamned saint. This country needs more than a miracle." I kept walking.

Stairs led down into the bar, and I had to duck under the stone door frame. The room smelled like a damp cave with deer trophies on the walls, thick wooden tables, and an uneven stone floor. Beata sat on a bench, her back against the stone wall, a glass and a bottle of vermouth in front of her. Tall and broad shouldered, her blond hair dark at the roots, she looked more German than Polish. She poured a glass for me.

"Finally, you are here." She held up the glass and smiled. "I thought you'd left town."

"Not without you," I joked, but I was partly serious.

During school breaks, Beata took me to castles and museums all over Poland—Wawel, Lublin, Olsztyn—where we filed past fragments of pottery, cracked friezes, and the Byzantine Christs that had been smuggled into Austria or whitewashed over during the war and then, much later, returned for restoration. I told myself that these Polish cities weren't much different from the town I grew up in, after the coal operators pulled out. Still, I depended on Beata's companionship and those trips we took away from our dreary town. We pretended to be tourists and made love in student hotels. Afterwards, as we tiptoed around the crushed wine bottles that drunken travelers had thrown against the hall shower drains,

I would often think nothing could remain whole in this country.

"Come with me to Czestochowa," I said. "I want to see the black Madonna."

"Why?" she asked. "You are not a good Catholic."

"Did I ever tell you what I did the first day of class? I pulled the crucifix down off the wall of the classroom and said, 'We'll have no more of this.'"

Beata turned pale. "But why?"

"I was thinking about Muslims, or people who don't believe in Christ. Why should they have to pray to a crucifix? My students were all terrified of me. It was a stupid thing to do. I know that now."

"Yes." She looked away from me.

"Everyone here looks like I do, but I don't think like them. I'll never think like you do, but at least if I go to the black Madonna, I might begin to understand. I've been asked to lead some pilgrims, two grandmothers, to Czestochowa. Will you come with me?"

"We'll go tomorrow night," she said.

I took a sip of the vermouth while she tossed back the rest of her wine. "Let me call my *babka* to tell her I won't be home."

Beata called her grandmother and her husband, Leszek. She called a taxi to take us to the train station. Once there, she bought two tickets to Warsaw where we would transfer to a bus headed for Czestochowa. I knew she didn't have much money, but when I offered her some *zloties*, she folded my hand back around the bills and said, "This makes me feel good too."

The next night, the second-class train compartment creaked and rocked like a cattle car. Some men stood outside the glass door and lit acidic Russian cigarettes, their smoke creeping back in to us through the compartment's vents. The two old women sat next to each other, across from Beata and me. I'd secretly named them Pani Red and Pani Holy Water. They unpacked Kielbasa and passed it to each other. They crammed plastic shopping bags labeled "Reklamowka" in the empty seats because they'd seen four Russian women on their way to the market, headed towards our compartment. I had seen hundreds of Russian peasants like these women with cracked teapots, army-issued night-vision goggles, tiny statues of Yuri Gagarin—all belongings they thought worth selling—stuffed in gym bags, climbing through train windows to catch the last trip to Warsaw or Krakow.

"*Czy wole?*" the peasants asked when they reached our compartment.

"*Nie.*" The old women shook their heads and patted their baggage. They held their noses and giggled after the peasants left. I looked down and pretended not to understand. The hot compartment smelled like heavy cigarette smoke, body odor, and kielbasa. I couldn't imagine it smelling any worse. They spoke in Polish, as though they thought I couldn't understand them if they spoke quickly, and, suddenly, I realized they were talking about me.

"He seems intelligent," Pani Holy Water said.

"Maybe," Pani Red said. "But why would he be here?"

"He must have been a bad priest. If he was good, he would not be sent here.

"They must have kicked him out of his last parish. He's here because he did something very bad, very bad."

"Have you heard about the priest from Bialystok? He made that young boy bleed to death."

"I thought you told them I wasn't a priest," I said to Beata.

"Yes, I did, but they are suspicious. They do not see how anyone but a holy man can live in a priest's house. It is the best house in our town."

"Say something to them," I said. "Tell them I understand everything they're saying."

Beata squeezed my hand under our jackets as I looked out the window. Angry and hopeless, I listened to the jagged, shushing sounds of Polish until we arrived in Warsaw.

I took them to the Pizza Hut in the basement of the Marriott Hotel in Central Warsaw where we ate a pizza that was so large it had to be propped up on a stand in the center of the table. I'd ordered sausage and pepperoni—without meat it would not have been a proper meal—but the holy women sat eyeing it suspiciously.

"He's rich," Pani Holy Water said. "Two kinds of meat."

"The priests are even wealthier in America." Pani Red sniffed her pizza and took a bite. "Give me the salt. This is tasteless." She dumped a fistful of salt onto her piece.

I had given Beata a pen and a notebook to practice her English. She listed her thoughts down the page as though she were conjugating verbs: "Sometimes I am so unhappy," she wrote. "I hate Pani Director. She always tell me what my life should be. I hate my job. I love my grandmother. I love English language. I love Americans."

I wondered why she hardly ever mentioned her husband. I'd met him once. Thin and unshaven, he looked twenty years older than Beata. He didn't rise from the couch during our visit. He read to me from Beata's English primer, a section on conjugating the verb "to rape." *I rape. I am being raped. I was raped. I will be raped.* As I turned to leave he told me there was no Polish word for "humor." Now, Beata stopped writing and pushed the paper and pen at me, then went to the line for drinks. She returned with two bottles of spring water.

"I am sorry, Christopher. Sometimes I think that you are from such a young, rich country and you have no problems, but I know this is not true. When I speak English, it is like I have a new voice to speak troubles I have in my heart for many years. I do not dare speak these things in Polish." She poured the carbonated water into a glass and held it to my lips.

"Why don't you leave if you hate it here?"

"Drink," she said, pushing her glass towards me. "It is spring water from sanitarium at Nalechow. It heals the heart."

Tasting the salt on the rim of the glass, I felt thirsty for a cool glass of plain water. Beata clutched her glass and gulped the water. Suddenly, I realized how little I knew about her. She took care of her grandmother; I knew that. She'd become sad when I asked her if she'd ever want to leave Poland. She said she'd lived in England with her husband two years before the fall of Communism. He'd taken a teaching position in Oxford. She had not spoken English then, and after a year of waiting everyday for her husband to come home from work, afraid to go out to buy milk, cheese and flowers from the market without him, she began crying. For weeks, she'd wept and no one could make her stop. Leszek gave up his job and took her back to Poland. She said she could never live that far from her country again, and she could not leave her husband. Sometimes, she looked at me as if I might disappear. I would some day, and I felt a pang of regret, or maybe love for her.

We took a southbound night bus packed with German tourists to Czestochowa. The orange tweed seats were stiff, with little leg room. The head-rest covers smelled like dirty hair. We stared through our reflections in the window at the lush pines, herds of cattle, and farms on the roadside. All around me, the Germans' words sounded familiar, like an English dialect that I could not understand.

The Czestochowa bus station was surrounded by a forest of smoky chimneys and cement buildings. It looked like a frozen city from inside the hot, dark bus. Shivering from fatigue and the night chill, we stepped onto the concrete and saw the light of Jasna Gora Monastery where the black Madonna was hidden behind a silver curtain. I began walking.

"Wait. You cannot see her now," Beata said.

"Why not?"

"You can only see her during a ceremony. You must wait until first mass at dawn."

In the bus station, the two old women sat on the bench and leaned towards each other, their rosaries woven between their fingers. I threw my jacket on the ground next to the bench and sat on it. Beata and I passed a bottle of vodka back and forth until she fell asleep with her head on my knee. She'd once told me that her husband would lay his head in her lap at night instead of making love to her, and that she felt more like a mother toward him than a wife. I touched her half-parted lips and pulled the loose strands of hair behind her ear. I wondered what this meant for her, to lay her head on my lap. I had begun to wish that I was the man she went home to every night.

At first light, we hiked to the monastery, but we could not see the madonna. Beata pulled me forward through the crowd towards a silver curtain on the altar. Then a brass band played a fanfare, and a curtain was lifted. The holy portrait had been dressed in emerald velvet cloth and white chrysanthemums. The madonna's pale hair was covered by a black veil with gilt fleur-de-lis, and a sword slash scarred her right cheek. Her face wasn't really black, but smudged with age and dirt. She frowned, her eyes sad and vacant. A few pilgrims hobbled around the shrine on their knees, and I imagined Agnieszka holding her swollen foot out to the madonna like an offering as her mother massaged the poison away with water and tears. I thought of Beata, alone in a dark Oxford flat, weeping for her conquered native country. Thick sweet incense swept through the church and gathered in the back of my throat. The old women knelt down on the stone floor and cried. I stood and swayed back on my heels with nausea, half wishing for a small vision or sign to tell me what I should do next. It was stifling in this church, like a hot, crowded museum, and I felt unholy standing there next to another man's wife. But I couldn't leave Beata. It seemed as though I no longer had a life in the country I'd left behind. My home was with her.

I sat down in an empty pew, too tired to stand. Just as I began to relax, someone grabbed me roughly by the arm and shook me. I turned to face a man scowling at me as he motioned towards Pani Holy Water, who was wobbling towards us on her swollen legs. The man was about the age of Beata's husband, unshaven, wearing a dingy engineer's cap and gray work trousers.

"Do I know you?" I asked in Polish.

"Why do you take a seat from an old woman?" he said.

"I didn't see her until now."

"Get up. Have some respect for a grandmother."

"There are plenty of open seats," I said.

He pulled me out of the pew and pushed me towards the door.

"Listen. You don't know me. I brought that old woman to see the black Madonna. I sat on the floor of the bus station so that she could sleep on a bench."

"You think you can come here to spend money and act rudely because you are a rich foreigner."

He sneered at me, leaned into my face and pulled on my arm again. I tried to push him off, and we became entwined in an awkward embrace, a boxer's stalemate, and I could smell the vodka on his hot breath. Finally, I pushed him away, and as I took a swing and knocked him over, I felt strangely weak as I watched him hit the floor, his head bouncing on the stone.

Beata took my arm and pulled me out into the market square. She sat down next to me on a bench, examined my arm for bruises and kissed me on both cheeks. When she saw that I wasn't hurt, she frowned at me.

"Shame on you," she said. "He has no education, no money, and maybe no home. He does not know better, but you have many years of education. You live in the richest place of our town. You know better than to behave that way. Shame. Shame on you."

I looked away from her, towards a group of fat pigeons shuffling around a garbage can. I knew that I would lose my mind soon if I didn't leave Poland, but I also knew that I must take Beata with me. I'd take her grandmother too, if necessary.

"Come with me to Prague," I said. "I've got to get out of this country. We'll go to Austria, and Italy, then London. Then I'll take you to see my home town."

She shook her head. "I cannot go with you, Christopher. Please do not ask me again."

She began walking back to the church, towards the two old women. She took Pani Red's elbow and carried Pani Holy Water's sweet-grass bag. Her head bent slightly forward, her shoulders hunched, she began to guide the women towards the bus station. My face burned as I watched her.

Father Tadeusz arrived at the rectory as we did. He sat in the cab of an army issued pick-up while Agnieska sat in the bed of the truck, one hand supporting the side of the freezer. He blew the horn and yelled,

"Christopher, we will have ice cubes now!"

I kissed Beata, knowing that she would not be with me the next time I left town. In my room, I composed a note to the school's director, a note I would leave with Beata in the library. It said, "My father is dying and I must go back to the States. I'm sorry for the inconvenience." I finished the bottle of Russian vodka that Father Tadeusz had given me. In the kitchen, I collected the radio, a hot plate, a French coffee press, my spoon, bowl and pot. I gathered them in my arms and carried them downstairs.

I was barefoot. I thought of all the pilgrims who bloodied their bare feet on broken wine bottles and rocks as they walked to the black Madonna. The mint-green hallway smelled of urine and of the iron from Polish tap water. The springs on Agnieszka's cot creaked as she rocked back and forth, placing communion-sized bites of German chocolate on her tongue. She smelled of chocolate and yeast, and as she leaned over to hide the candy, I saw that the back of her head was nearly bald. She sat in the center of the mattress, a brown wool blanket draped around her like the robes of the black Madonna. I knelt before this ruined creature and she moved like a shadow, her shaking fingers touching the radio, the hot plate, and then my face. I bowed my head to her and asked her to save me.

Stoics

My husband loves my reticence.
He says stoicism is underrated in women.
His mother can tolerate more pain than any other human being.
Her tailbone broke with his birth
breaking again with the last of five children.
She had no friends, needed
only her children.
She told no one
until the breast tumor grew to the size of a baby's fist.
Unfavored daughter, she drove alone up the mountain,
past her young, favored brother's grave
to warn her own mother of the surgery.

My husband buys his mother soft winter hats she never wears.
He takes me to the brick house kettled between two mountain ridges,
where she sits at the kitchen table in a white robe, unashamed
of her perfect baldness,
her chemo-burned skin clear and white as Saint Catherine's lilies.
Quiet, I sit across from her,
watching for signs of weakness.
She eats, testing out country ham, chess pie
on her chemo-cracked tongue.
Outside the window, my husband tunnels through thick winter snow on
his belly
our son, his nephews stacked on his back.
Snow clouds pour over the mountain ridge
their shadows spilling, gliding over his white path like dark wings.

Afraid of crying, I take myself away from her.
Upstairs in my husband's childhood bed, I think of stoics.
Stoical stoically
In Latin, stoicus means the porch of Zeno,
Greek philospher who asked the old question:
Whether it were better to have moderate affections or no affections
The stoics said none.
Patient endurance indifference
to pleasure or pain
rigor asceticism
stoique in France, stoico in Italy, Sienna, lascivious home
of Saint Catherine, the most austere mystic.
At sixteen, she cut off her luxurious golden hair,
scalded herself at the source of a hot spring,
caught small pox,
scrubbing the scabs raw and bleeding
until she was ugly, old enough to wear the white veil
of the widowed mantellata.
Catherine's mother had no use for her daughter's heroics,
made her into a servant
until she fell into the kitchen fire,
burning with exquisite visions.
Her father saw the white doves above her head,
gave her away to the Dominicans
who taught her to regard the sweet as bitter,
the bitter as sweet.

My husband appears in the doorway,
his face fallen with gentle grief.
"How is she?" I ask. "What does she need?"
Below us,
his mother wants nothing,
asks for nothing.

My whole body aches
beneath the weight of her grace.
I recall how she laughed as she told him over the phone of her latest
dream:
I'm standing on the front porch in a hurricane
in my mastectomy bra
No matter how hard I try to hold on
the bra's lace and batting tears out with the wind, rising
like doves through the rain.

The Worst Thing I'll Ever Do to You

Although I'd given birth three days before, my mother wanted to tell me about her stillborn children.

"It felt like someone had tied my insides together with a rope," she said. "Then they tied the other end to a horse and slapped the horse on the rear."

"I can't listen to this right now," I said.

"Both of them died in the birth canal. One a year before you and one a few years after. Right before you were born, the doctor lost your heartbeat. I thought you'd died too, Anna."

I held the bedpost as she wound the ace bandages around my swollen chest. She yanked tightly, nearly pulling me off my feet, and I winced at the pressure that would stop the milk from flowing uncontrollably when I heard my son, Jacob, cry.

"He sure is a buster," my mother said, looking into the bassinet.

I looked down too. Jacob was so alive, so hungry that he'd nursed until my breasts were engorged, and I'd become feverish. I'd just given up nursing the day my mother flew up from Charleston to my home in Travelers Rest, and my husband, Christopher, fed Jacob his first bottle as we waited for her arrival. The infection in my chest stung so badly that I could not hold him, so I sat in the next room, wondering what comfort I could give my child now that I could not pull him close for nourishment. I'd cried as the wasted milk rolled down to my navel, and I hoped that I'd be able to pull myself together enough to smile and yell, "Here comes the cavalry," by the time my mother stepped out of the taxi.

"They're going to kick me out of the La Leche League," I said, my voice shaking again.

"Don't get so upset," she said. "A lot of women can't nurse. Why do you think they invented formula?"

My mother helped me put my flannel shirt back on.

"I've come to cook, clean and run errands," she said. "You'll take

65

care of your baby. Newborns make me nervous."

I called my mother Rose Marie because she didn't always answer to "mother." She pulled each silver strand from her cropped black hair; she used a young girl's voice when she talked to my husband. My father, who died during his third bypass surgery, was a tall, lanky man who liked to rest his elbow on the top of her head whenever they stood next to each other. He'd called Rose Marie a high maintenance woman. As a child, I assumed this meant she had brittle bones; her wrist broke when she played tennis, and her tail bone broke three times—once from a slip on ice and then twice from the pressures of birth.

By our second day together, I began sending Rose Marie on errands to the grocery for floor wax and to the hardware store for plant hangers. I didn't really need these things, but it made her feel good to fix up my house, and I would do anything to keep her from feeling bored or morose and begin telling stories about her lost children. I'd lost a semester's pay because I taught adjunct composition classes at three of the local colleges. Living on Christopher's salary from managing a bookstore, we were going broke funding Rose Marie's trips to the market.

I followed Christopher out onto the driveway as he left for work. We rented a two-story brick house on a lonely gravel road, about two miles from a small airport. Pines with thin barren trunks surrounded and leaned over our house, dropping sap on our parked cars. The sap looked like rain on the windshields, and it had to be scraped off daily with fingernails, razor blades, or credit cards.

"Don't let her fix anything in the house," he said. "That's why we pay rent."

I picked the pine needles from the windshield of his Subaru and scraped at the sap on the glass. Christopher had once said the only reason he would leave me would be because of my mother.

"You have to pull yourself together and stand up to her," he said. "You're too easy to push around when you're unhappy."

I was struggling with postpartum blues and the fear that I would never love my son properly. I felt anxiety, wonder, but not love—at least not the way it was shown in parenting books. I'd grown to hate those magazine pictures of young women with flawless skin and thick braids down their backs, nursing their calm infants, smiling euphorically as they kissed their children's tiny feet. Even while Jacob slept, I paced aimlessly around the house in unwashed maternity pants and my husband's flannel shirts, which were always damp from my leaking chest. I forgot laundry in the washer for two days until it soured. I left a can of soup cooking on the range for three hours and offered it to Christopher as though it were still good. I cried when he left for work in the morning and then again in the evening when he returned. At night, I read about pneumonia, croup and projectile vomiting in my child care book and wept over the illnesses my son might contract. One day, Christopher told me he'd rented *A Long Day's Journey Into Night*, and I cried at this too, remembering what a sad movie it had been the last time we'd watched it.

I watched Christopher drive off, and then I walked slowly toward our house. The moss rose had been singed by the early September heat, and the impatiens drooped in the window boxes. Climbing up to the porch, I noticed a brick had fallen from the steps and was lying in the flower bed. I grabbed the front doorknob and it wouldn't turn—the door had locked automatically from the inside. I rang the bell and then remembered that Rose Marie must be in the shower. Jacob had been napping before I left the house, but now I imagined his cries. My shirt became moist and the skin beneath my bandages began to itch. I panicked. It was as if our separation had never occurred at birth; our bodies still worked in the same rhythms. I needed to hold him, and I wondered what the ache to hold a dead infant must feel like. I picked up the brick, ran around to the back of the house and pulled the screen aside. I considered throwing the brick through the kitchen window. Then Rose Marie moved into view as she scrubbed her coffee cup in the sink. I knocked on the glass, and she opened it.

"Why didn't you unlock the door when I knocked?" I asked.

"I was making a list," she said. "I'm going to buy new locks for your doors."

"The old ones work fine," I said.

"What if you get locked out of the house with Jacob all alone inside the house with those cats? A cat will suck the breath from a baby."

"That's an old wives' tale," I said. "And I'm not getting rid of my cats, if that's what you're suggesting."

I felt too weak to fight her. Before Rose Marie arrived, I'd been living like a nocturnal animal, eating only bites of oatmeal and catching twenty minutes of rest between Jacob's two-hour feedings. Often, I couldn't sleep while he napped, so I child-proofed the house. Just the thought of dropping Jacob on the hearth sent me running to the cedar chest for blankets and pillows that I layered on top of the bricks and secured with twine to the legs of the wood-burning stove.

"I guess it would save Christopher some time if we called the landlord," I said.

The landlord said he'd reimburse me for the locks, so we swaddled Jacob in three receiving blankets, propped him up with pillows in his stroller, and walked to the hardware store.

"You look better already," Rose Marie said. "You need to get out some."

My son looked tiny and fragile outside. His life seemed so delicate, and my fear of failing him, constant. While I was pregnant, Rose Marie had told me stories about clumps of blood in the toilet bowl, of placenta previa, of knots in the umbilical cord. Because of Rose Marie's warnings, I'd spent my pregnancy believing that at least one dead child or difficult birth was a prerequisite for a healthy newborn. As I pushed the stroller, I talked about my son's healthy birth because it felt good to prove my mother wrong, and because giving birth was all I could think about. I'd been lonely for another woman's company, a mother's comfort, but now that she was here, I resented her because I didn't feel any better.

"It wasn't that bad," I said. I'd felt calm when my water broke. I felt formidable as I collected my toothbrush. I wasn't worried. All I could think about were the names of my next four children and that I'd be losing two quarts of amniotic fluid as Christopher gathered beach towels for me to sit on in the car.

"When you called me and said you were in labor and then I didn't hear from you all night, I nearly went crazy with worry," Rose Marie said.

I'd called her from the labor room and held the phone out so that she could hear the Doppler rhythm of my son's heart, loud as a helicopter landing.

"We never lost his heartbeat," I said proudly. "It just kept getting louder."

I didn't tell her that after fifteen hours of labor, when the contractions slammed into the bottom of my spine, I thought my leg would break off from my groin. I didn't tell her that I'd remembered how she once told me that when she was young, the only time they kept women awake for childbirth was when they delivered stillborns, and I'd wondered how she had withstood this pain for something that was already dead. I'd tried to reason with the doctor. "Couldn't you just put me to sleep and wait until tomorrow for this? I worked all day. I'm too tired to give birth tonight." The doctor was dressed all in white and scrubbed pink; even his scalp shone through the strands of hair on his forehead. He'd looked like a newborn, and at that moment, I'd needed him more than I'd ever needed my own husband.

Walt's Hardware was in a mostly vacant strip mall. Walt was a short, balding man who kept two of everything in his store—two hurricane lamps, two hoses, two bags of bird seed. The cash register rang as he stalked the aisles, telling customers that if he didn't have it, he'd order it for them. As we walked through the store, it occurred to me that when I'd given birth, as when I'd visited my father in the hospital, everyone around me had kept moving while I remained still. I felt, as I had after my father's long sickness, like I'd been beaten up and left on the side of a busy highway like an old punctured tire.

"Well hello, big feller," Walt said to Jacob. Then he smiled at my mother. "What am I going to sell you two lovely young ladies today?"

"My daughter needs new door locks," Rose Marie said in her young girl's voice. "One of these days, she'll lock herself out, and this helpless infant will be left all alone inside."

"We can't let that happen. Just give me a few minutes, and I'll put the locks in for you."

"That's okay," I said. "My husband can install them."

"Will it cost extra for the installment?" Rose Marie asked.

"Only if you don't tell me your name," he said.

"My name is Rose Marie." My mother giggled, and I felt embarrassed for her.

As Walt went to the back of the store, my mother glanced around garden supplies and found two brass doorknobs. She blew off that gritty dust which covers things that have never been moved. She checked her lipstick in the reflection on the brass. She knew that a newborn inspired the promptest and friendliest service from people. She must have been counting on this when Walt returned with his tool belt.

"Do you have any other locks in the back?" she asked. "These don't have a dead bolt."

"I could order some for you, but it'll take six weeks," he said.

"These will be fine," I said.

Walt kept an infant seat in the bed of his pickup. He swung it out of the bed and strapped Jacob into the back seat. As he helped me into the back, I could smell whiskey and cigarettes on his breath. He took Rose Marie's arm, lifted her into the front of the cab and pulled the seat belt over her, lingering a while before he let it click.

"That car seat was my daughter's," he said. "She's ten years old now."

"I'll bet she's a daddy's girl," Rose Marie said.

"She lives in Montana with her mother," he said. "Her mother lets me see her on Christmas. I wake up on Christmas morning and cook and fill the house with the smell of ham and eggs. Once a year, I'm the daddy again. I get to yell to my wife and daughter, 'Hey, girls, breakfast is ready.'"

"I know how you feel," Rose Marie said. "I'm only here on a visit. My grandson probably won't know who I am."

"Oh, he'll know you," I said. I turned to Walt. "Were you in the room when your daughter was born?"

"She was a home birth," Walt said. "I had to cut the umbilical cord and bury the placenta in our garden. As I stood over her with a Swiss army knife, I said to her, 'I hope this is the worst thing I'll ever do to you.'

I felt like I'd just severed her from the Garden of Eden."

We bounced up the gravel road and parked next to the house. Walt helped my mother out and then offered an arm to me. Rose Marie showed Walt where to go and then pointed up the stairs.

"Go take a nap, Anna. I'll cook supper," she said. "You've got to learn how to sleep when he sleeps."

Her mothering surprised me sometimes. When I was six, after the last stillborn, she'd begun locking herself in the bathroom for five or six hours at a time. Perhaps her body had made sense to her, as mine had, when she was pregnant. Every part had a new function—skin and muscles gave way to the growing uterus, joints loosened and pelvis bone softened for the baby's movement through the birth canal. After the stillbirth, she must have felt unbearably empty when she looked in the bathroom mirror and discovered the red stretch marks beneath her sagging abdomen, or traced the linea nigra, the brown line of pigment that ran from her rib cage down through her navel, splitting her in half. With no child to nurse, she must have healed more slowly, bled longer. Once, she locked herself in the bathroom, and I'd curled up and slept on the floor outside the door. She'd left banana bread in the oven until I could smell its charred remains. I discovered that she was brushing her hair mercilessly because I found clumps of it in the sink when my father returned home from selling business forms and night school and opened the bathroom door to let me in. When she smelled what had burned, my mother ran into the kitchen, screaming, "That hateful child just sat there and let my bread burn. She does it because she hates me. You both do it because you hate me."

A few days after the burned-bread incident, I'd found wine-colored stains on the bathroom rug. I soaked my washcloth with cold water and began to scrub at them until I felt my mother kneel beside me, as at the communion rail in church. She gently pulled the rag from my hand.

"You shouldn't have seen this," she said, then leaned against the tub. She looked pale and weak, and it frightened me. I backed away from her.

71

"I would have named this one Charles," she said, sitting up again. "Your father wanted to name you that even after we knew you were a girl, but I wouldn't let him."

Now, I listened to Rose Marie brown the Italian sausage and spice it with oregano, basil and fennel. I promised myself that I would never lock my son out of any room. I could hear her talking happily, and I hoped this meant that Walt was working on the doors. It also saddened me to think of how eager she was to befriend strangers.

Jacob sneezed, and I heard a rattle in his throat. He sneezed once more, and I called the pediatrician. Dr. Finn was doing rounds at the hospital, but the nurse said if it would make me feel better, I could bring Jacob over to outpatient services.

I wasn't supposed to drive yet, but I grabbed my keys, lifted Jacob from the bed and walked quietly down the stairs. It had rained the night before, and the mallards from the park had waddled into our yard to float in the puddles. Two brown swallows flew out of the pines behind our shed, twirling around each other, and I couldn't tell if they were mating or fighting. As I backed my Ford out of the driveway, I looked at the house. Three hanging ferns, large as prehistoric jungle plants, took over the porch and hid the wooden swing. The flower beds were lined with seashells and the base of each pine was circled with smooth river rocks. From a distance, my home looked like a child's drawing of a gingerbread house, filled with perfect people.

A nurse named Jeanette met me in the outpatient services. She led me into an examination cubicle and pulled the curtain closed. She was old and brittle, but she wore a soft, pink medical jacket. She held Jacob like a football and called him "Mister."

"All newborns sneeze," she said. "Mr. Jacob is just clearing out the stuff from birth. Turn on his humidifier tonight."

I couldn't talk because I knew I would start sobbing with relief.

"Once you get to know him, you'll figure things out. I have eight children. When they were young, I remember being buried beneath children—two grabbing my legs, one strapped to my chest, and the other under my arm like this, and I could still fold laundry and stir the gravy."

After my last child was born, I sat up and said, 'I feel fine, thank you. All I need is a warm shower and some lunch.' "

"I just want to keep him safe," I said. "I don't know how I'm going to do that."

She reached over and pulled the hair out of my eyes. "You're doing fine. He's stronger than you think. The only way you can hurt him is if you throw him down and step on him, and your motherly instincts won't allow that to happen."

I wondered why I hadn't met this woman when I was pregnant. Walking past the gift shop, I remembered that my father had died in a small hospital like this one. The night before his surgery, Rose Marie and I had stood on either side of his bed, watching *Jeopardy*. My father had been given morphine for his chest pains. We couldn't watch him, and he couldn't watch the TV.

"I want an open casket and a New Orleans Jazz band," he'd said. "You can cover me with ice and cold boiled shrimp. Then I want you to place a bowl of cocktail sauce in my hands so that the mourners can all dip their shrimp when they come to view my body."

Rose Marie left the room.

"You won't die," I said. "Who'll take care of Rose Marie?" We could joke about her now that I was older.

"I can't work. I won't make the money she's used to," he said. "I'm afraid she doesn't want me anymore."

"I can't listen to this," I said. "Just stop talking and rest."

"It's best that I die first," he said.

When I got home from the hospital, Christopher was sitting on the front porch, his jacket and bag lying next to him. He was reading the paper and as he looked up, my stomach fluttered.

"You shouldn't have been driving," he said.

"I thought the baby was sick," I said. "I took him to the hospital. Why are you out here?"

"My key won't open the door," he said. "Do you know why?"

"Why didn't you ring the bell?"

73

"The car was gone. I thought you were out somewhere."

I tried my old key for his benefit, to delay his disappointment.

"It was the only thing I asked you to do," he said. "Please don't let her fix things."

"You wanted the locks changed. I wanted them changed, too. Walt came right when we asked him, and he didn't charge us to install them."

"I wanted to be the one to change the locks. I live here. She doesn't."

"She likes fixing things for us. It makes her feel needed."

"When you're a guest in someone's house, you don't just change the things you don't like."

"Just humor her."

"Your father humored her for twenty-five years. Look where it got him. If you don't tell her to stop it, I will."

"I can't deal with you two right now."

"If you don't tell her, I'll leave right now," he said.

"Fine," I said. "Leave."

Our fights always ended with his leaving. Our last fight, when I was eight months pregnant, began when I asked him if he'd want to be pregnant and endure the pain of labor if he could. He'd said no, that he was glad it was me instead of him, so I locked myself in the bedroom. He'd driven out to the airport, where he'd fallen asleep in his car. He said he awoke when a plane flew over and the car rocked gently. On his way back the next morning, he'd bought a plastic swimming pool, a peace offering. He filled it with hose water warmed by the late August sun. We both stripped down to our sunglasses and sat side-by-side, our legs crossed over each other's.

"I thought I was going to be hit out there," he'd said. "I thought I was dead."

"What if I were dying from childbirth, and you could save the baby or me. Who would you save?" I'd asked.

"They always save the mother first," he'd said. "Besides, I wouldn't let you die and leave me to take care of a newborn."

74

Now, he stood and put on his jacket. He walked down to his car. Suddenly I wanted him to leave for good and to take our son with him. I wanted to start my adult life over, before I could make all the painful mistakes of motherhood.

I rang the doorbell and sat on the porch step, waiting for Rose Marie to let me into my house. After my father died, I'd blamed her for his weak heart. At his funeral, I told her never to call me. She began clipping articles from the newspaper and mailing them to me. According to the clippings, whole families could be wiped out in car crashes, and babies died from polluted batches of Cheerios. Five years passed. Then one Christmas, she'd flown from Charleston to my home with a thirty-pound turkey in her carry-on bag. She'd baked it all night, waking every two hours to baste it with whiskey and apple preserves. She'd wrapped it in foil and dishtowels so that it would stay warm during the plane trip. She let herself into my house, set the turkey on the table and began heating gravy. "I always cook the bird," was all she said.

Rose Marie peeked through the curtains and flung the front door open. She'd tied Christopher's apron over her silk blouse, and her hair was curled from cooking steam. For the first time, I noticed, she'd allowed it to turn gray. There was a red slash on her cheek, and beneath it was purple.

"Where did you go? Where were you?" she said as I walked past her. It looked like an amateur thief had ransacked the kitchen but found nothing worth taking. The pan of spaghetti sauce was overturned on the floor, and wads of paper towels were lying on top of the sauce.

"What happened in here?"

"He tried to touch me," she said. "I fell."

"Who touched you? Walt?"

She nodded.

"Did you call the police?"

"Of course not. He just got the wrong signals. That's all."

She looked haggard, disheveled, no longer the formidable and pretty woman I remembered. Watching her, I understood how unfair I'd been to blame her for my father's death; he'd had a diseased heart, and she'd lost him. Then she'd lost me for five years. Now, she was a lonely, aging woman.

"I'm sorry," she said.

"I'm not angry with you," I said. I unwrapped my son, heated his bottle and began to feed him. He gulped air and twisted in my arms, trying to latch onto the nipple. It wasn't much different from nursing. I looked away from her, down at my son. I thought about the day that inevitably would come, when I would punish Jacob for running into the street in front of a speeding truck, or for swimming in the neighbor's pool without my permission. My son would say, "I hate you," those words I dreaded most, and I felt a rush of loneliness that only mothers understand, and for a moment, I let myself forget all the contentions I had with my own mother.

"Why don't you hold your grandson," I said. "He's really not that fragile. You won't hurt him."

I passed my son into my mother's lap and watched him as he startled for a moment against her frail arms.

"Wait," she said. "This doesn't feel right. I've got to feed him with the other hand."

She shifted him across her chest. Then he settled in and started to take long, complete swallows, as slowly as some forms of forgiveness.

Aubade

All night drowsing
on a balcony woven with jasmine,
I've watched the butcher's daughter
beautifully seduce
the grocer's son. Playing
Clytemnestra to his Agamemnon,
the girl shimmers before candles
in sea shells that stage her
inside this cliff town's market place.
Below the clock tower,
she floats her robe across cobblestone,
beckons her wayward husband to cross
silk into fatal bath.
Her loveliness tyrannizes
the eyes of retired stone masons
swigging grappa beside the war memorial.
They hunch toward each other
as if to whisper,
We are not dead, we are not yet cold.
The clock tower chimes seven. Full of sleep
I believe I can fall
safely into graves
one hundred feet below.
The north wind rouses
jasmine's thick perfume.
An autobus hums
on an unseen street. I linger
between beauty and movement.
Larks unfold

over poppies flaming
in the canyon.
The masons rise, saunter
toward wives hanging empty bed sheets
over fortress walls
to purify
in wind and sunlight.

The Flight Patterns of Birds

We knew Donald Maclain was a former spy who once escaped from a Makhabarat prison because he owned a rapier given to him for service to the Queen of England. Now that he'd retired from British Naval Intelligence, the basket-handled sword leaned against a bookshelf in the library of his winter home south of Edinburgh. Early March through September, Donald worked as an explosives expert with my husband, Christopher, supervising a machine that dredged up silt from the bottom of the Gulf Coast. When he came home from work, Christopher often spoke of his older friend's virtues with a boyish awe. He said Donald was an expert on falconry and gourmet cooking; he could locate the best curry in restaurants throughout Florida, Alabama, Louisiana, Texas and Mississippi. The November my husband took medical leave for a retinal occlusion that blinded his right eye, Donald invited us to visit him in Scotland. As we stood outside our hotel on Princes Street, waiting for Donald to come take us out of the city, Christopher said his friend's most impressive skill was his ability to blend in.

"The best spies look like somebody's bachelor uncle," he said. "That way, they don't arouse suspicion." I stepped toward the street corner, hoping to catch a glimpse of Donald. Christopher threw his hand in front of my chest.

"Wait," he said. "I want to see how long it takes us to spot him."

A current of early Christmas shoppers pushed around us on the wet, black pavement. While my husband scanned the crowd, I rubbed my cold hands together, surveyed the castle across the street. When we'd arrived the night before its medieval walls were backlit by floodlights, glowing as brightly as the Ferris wheel that spun below in the street market. That morning, the castle and its heather gardens were bleached by late November frost. A short man with a flushed complexion and close-cropped gray hair grabbed Christopher's shoulder and kissed my cheek. When he gathered us both into his wool coat, his day-old beard grazed my chin, and I smelled cigars and a cologne as bittersweet as chrysanthemums.

"Anna, you remember Donald?" Christopher said.

"I hope I haven't kept you waiting," Donald said, lifting our luggage. He directed us to a tiny, black Volkswagon Gulf parked on the street. "Let's get out of this dreadful city."

Donald settled our bags in the luggage rack and waved us inside the car. I offered to sit in back so that Christopher could catch up with Donald, but after the initial pleasantries, the men fell quiet while Donald expertly negotiated the confusing roundabouts on the road leading out of the city. Christopher picked up a copy of *The Daily Record* from the floor, rubbed his bad eye and squinted at the small print instead of looking out the window. At thirty-eight, Christopher was the youngest patient his doctor had ever seen with a retinal occlusion, a form of blindness caused, in my husband's case, by a blood clot that shot from a hole in his heart. The doctor told us that most people lived long, healthy lives with holes in their hearts, oblivious to them. He said that the clot that found its way into Christopher's eye had been the result of plain, dumb luck. When we asked him what my husband could do to prevent another clot from shooting into his other eye, or someplace worse, the doctor lowered his own eyes to write a prescription for blood thinners and said, "If I were you I'd travel, see some things."

After Donald's invitation, Christopher immediately booked round trip tickets to Edinburgh and plotted out our trip using three different guide books, highlighting the castles, museums and churches he wanted to see. Though he'd never traveled anywhere in Europe north of London, he claimed the pictures of rugged Scottish landscapes reminded him of the mountains in Virginia, the geography of his childhood. But lately he seemed to be grieving the sound of lost words more than mountain vistas. The night we packed for this trip, I'd found him sitting on the floor between the bookshelf and the piano, his long legs spread out beneath the piano bench. His high school textbook, *Adventures in English Literature*, was in his lap, open to Tennyson's "In Memoriam."

"Listen," he said, reading a stanza. "I loved this when I was a kid."

Christopher made me swear to tell no one back home in South Carolina about his failing sight; I kept his secret because I hadn't yet figured out how to explain it to anyone. I couldn't think about it too long or too deeply without falling to pieces, and so far, keeping myself together had been the only thing my husband needed of me. But as I watched him hesitate an extra second before focusing on the tabloid on the bus, I dreaded his blindness. I wondered why, now that we'd traveled all this way, Christopher stubbornly refused to admire this splendid city. Turning toward the window, I willed my husband to look with me. A wild-haired man stood on the street corner, his face painted blue like William Wallace, playing a Scottish lament on the bagpipes. I felt an ancient, familiar fatigue, as though we were travel-worn pilgrims who'd lost sight of our holy destination.

Outside the city, row houses gave way to the green and gold Pentland Hills rolling in the distance. As we passed through an old coal town, I looked through the picture windows of pebble-dash bungalows that lined the road, trying to see the people inside. I counted a surprising number of Italian restaurants and spotted a tavern sign that read, "We serve pizza and potatoes." When I nudged Christopher's shoulder, he looked up dreamily from his paper.

"The Snap-On Tool man was murdered in this village last week," he said.

"They found his truck abandoned in an empty parking lot," Donald said.

"Did they find his body?" I asked.

"No."

"Then how do they know he was murdered if they didn't find his body?"

"I don't know, Anna," Christopher said. "It says here that all his tools were stolen."

Christopher looked back to his newspaper, and we didn't speak as Donald drove through the main street of Rosslyn, passing the old inn and the new inn, turning onto the road that led past a weathered, yellow field house, stopping before a wrought iron cemetery gate.

"This is it." Donald lifted our luggage and offered his hand to me as I stepped out of the back seat.

It was colder on Donald's property. The winter sun had fallen behind the forest, casting the hawthorns and pines before us in a pale, blue light. Along the gravel drive, I stepped over the crystallized maple leaves at our feet, listening to Donald explain how his grandmother had grown up in the glen below the castle, working in the ammunitions factory. Donald could remember hiding in the caves beneath the castle when war planes passed over the village when he was a boy. After the war, Donald said, the cottages in the glen had been razed, the surrounding forest restored to its wild, natural state. Now that Donald rented the castle from the Landmark Trust every fall, he could name the deer, foxes and owls hidden in the trees along the path. He said he'd acquired a trained Harris hawk the last time he was in Houston. He'd named her Isis.

We turned at a bend and saw a small, square castle on top a sandstone cliff, the pink walls of its ruins burnished by the golden, setting sun. To the right of the house, fog rose from the waters of the North Esk, billowing up from the glen into the white feathery hawthorns, and I mistook all the whiteness for an iced-over lake. Donald pushed open the heavy front door and led us into a warm, carpeted entrance way. A short, pot-bellied pine sat in the far corner, red and gold ribbons wrapped around the lowest branches, trailing off to the floor. The smell of curries wafted from the kitchen.

"I may need your help with the Christmas greenery," Donald said, nodding at the unfinished tree.

Up a narrow staircase and down a hallway, we stopped in the doorway of a small red office. Inside, a smooth, white desk was pushed against the far wall, its surface crowded with a cross-platform computer, telephone, digital camera, fax and scanner. Above the black office equipment hung a painting of a nude. The color of dark earth, she was lying on her side, her arms crossed over her breasts and bound at the wrists by thorny vines. She was so beautiful and disturbing that I had to look away.

"What a red room," I said quickly. "What do you call this shade of red?"

"I believe it's called brick," Donald said, herding us towards the end of the hallway.

The guest room was painted all white, filled with a high, carved walnut bed with a plaster of Paris crown hanging on the wall above its headboard. The enormous bed left room only for a small vanity table that fit into the bare, recessed window at its foot. The other three walls of the guest room were covered with charcoal sketches of a young, nineteenth century woman caught in different states of repose.

"Dinner will be served at eight," Donald said, turning abruptly.

I flopped on the bed as Christopher unpacked our white noise machine, placing it on the bed stand.

"I can't believe you carried that all this way," I said, though secretly I was relieved to see it. He'd bought it the summer before to cover street noises with the sounds of a waterfall, a tropical forest, a summer rain. I preferred the pure white noise, but Christopher insisted on listening to the running stream, and the machine had been the source of petty, bedtime arguments. Lately, neither of us could sleep without it.

"We forgot to bring a gift," I said.

"You can walk down to the village," he said. "I saw a liquor store on our way in."

"Want to come with me?"

He pulled a thin flashlight from his suitcase. "You'll need this." He turned on the white noise machine and lay across the bed with his hiking boots still on, crossing his arm over his eyes.

I first met Donald eight years before, when he and Christopher began supervising the S.I.L.T project. The dredging machine, which was called "The Wing," broke down often and required Christopher to travel from our Carolina mill town to all the port cities where he worked with Donald in spring and summer. When I wasn't teaching, I sometimes went with him on his business trips. One early March evening, a storm on its way, Christopher, Donald and I sat in an open air restaurant on Royale Street in New Orleans as a ceiling fan pushed the warm, damp air above our heads. Donald seemed to have a genuine interest in my graduate dissertation on the Hindu tradition of suttee. He listened attentively while I explained that for some Hindu women the act of burning themselves alive was akin to the sacrifices of Christian martyrs. I told him how I'd struggled to overcome my own revulsion to the tradition, transcending it in order to study the Hindu widow's concept of what it meant to live on after her husband's death.

We'd had a few cocktails before dinner and after a while began comparing our unfortunate driver's license photos. Donald leaned close, opened his wallet. At first I thought he was showing me the pink glare of his forehead captured at the DMV, but it was his license to carry a concealed weapon. He told me how he once spent nine months in a Makhabarat prison in Baghdad near the end of the Iran Contra scandal. While his captors starved him to a third of his body weight, he imagined whole menus at restaurants like the one where we were eating.

"In solitary, I ran the menus of every restaurant I'd ever eaten in through my mind, every course, every piece of linen, every candle, even the color of the wallpaper. Whenever I felt dangerously close to self pity, I invented characters to sit at those restaurant tables, and I played their stories like soap operas in my head. I wasn't afraid when they came to question me. I resented the intrusion."

"How did you get over it?" I asked. "After you were released.?"

He unbuttoned his shirt to reveal his bare collar bone. "They set my broken collar bone, replaced my missing teeth. I went through physical therapy."

He hadn't answered my question, but his eyes were dark and distant, and I was afraid to ask him anything else. We'd met a handful of times after that, but when Christopher phoned him with news of his illness, Donald invited us to come visit with him. He said he had plenty of room because his wife was visiting her family in Wales.

Despite Donald's astonishing generosity, he unnerved me. His painful history loomed beneath the surface of our encounters, and I never learned how to make small talk with him. Walking down the hallway of his home, I passed the red room filled with office equipment. In the dim light, it seemed as though Donald were conducting surveillance over something much graver than oil or silt. Near the half-decorated pine in the foyer, I heard his bass voice coming from the kitchen.

"The bits and pieces belong in the center of the table, Margaret," he scolded. "This isn't just a meal. It's a production."

I stood in the doorway of the pale, yellow kitchen, my face and hands warmed by the gas stove. A slim girl with a single brown braid rushed past me, nodding, carrying a tray of finger bowls filled with dried dates, banana slices and cashews out to the dining room. The kitchen smelled of the allspice and anise seeds that were crushed and scattered around the mortar and pestle on the center island. Donald stood over the range at the end of the island, flattening balls of nan, dropping them into a pan of spitting grease.

"How is he?" Donald asked.

"He doesn't want to look at anything," I said.

"What do you think he should see?"

"Castles," I said. "Vistas. I thought we could hike to the top of Arthur's Seat and look out over the city." I paused, suddenly aware that I had no idea what my husband should be seeing. "What would you be looking at?"

"Well, I suppose if I were going blind, I'd take in every strip bar on Bourbon Street." I laughed, feeling hollow. When Donald looked straight into my eyes, I clenched my hands. The dough sputtered in the grease. "How are you holding out?"

My stomach sank and a bitter thickness rose into the back of my throat. Lately, I'd grown accustomed to my husband's quiet melancholy, our new life of hospital waiting rooms, indifferent doctors. I could take all the bad blind man jokes in the world from this man, but I couldn't bear his unexpected kindness. Looking away from his eyes, I ground the already crushed spices with the pestle.

"I'm fine," I said. "Just don't be so nice to me."

"Despite what your husband may have told you about me, I can

85

be kind," he said.

"I know. The only thing I can't seem to handle right now is kindness."

"Okay, then. Please leave my kitchen so that I may finish." He handed me the flashlight I'd set on the counter. "Don't forget your torch."

Christopher once told me that a sunset takes a half hour, the exact time it takes for the eyes to adjust to darkness. I tested his theory as I walked the twilit country road though the graveyard and into the village. At the edge of town, street lamps glowed white against the black sky and the nearly deserted sidewalks. In the street-corner liquor store, an elderly clerk limped out from behind the counter, stood very close and peered directly into my face. The left side of his mouth pulled lower than the right, and his left arm bent uselessly against his side. He spoke English, but I barely understood him. He swept his good arm back and forth before a neat row of rum and vodka behind the cash register, and I determined that he was pointing out a sale on Bacardi. Where was all the Scotch whiskey? I shook my head and thanked him. As I grew used to his thick accent, I realized that he was asking a question.

"I'm sorry," I said. "I didn't catch what you just said."

"Oh, I thought you were from here," he said.

"I flew in from South Carolina yesterday."

He bowed slightly and smiled. "Ah, the center of the universe."

"I'm staying at the castle."

He glanced at the neat row of rum bottles behind the cash register. "Are there many Americans living up at the castle?"

"Just the two of us and our host. He's Scottish. We're going to see the sites in Edinburgh."

"Dreadful city. I hardly go there if I can help it."

I bought a bottle of Frascati and a Tuscan red. Then I bought a bottle of discounted rum and five dark chocolate bars. Loaded down with bottles and chocolates, I stepped outside, looked toward the black road I'd taken into town. There weren't any street lamps in the cemetery. Regretting my rash flight from Donald's estate, I stood at the end of the drive, the cold burning my lungs and sinuses. I put the bag of liquor and chocolate down and held out my free hand to test the flashlight. My hand wavered in the fragile beam. Ahead of me, the black graveyard gate had swung open. Tombstones lined the hillside like carefully placed chess pieces, a cold and constant wind blowing over and around them, muting out all natural sound. Donald's hawk could be perched in a pine beside the drive, its unseen eyes upon me; the Snap-on Tool man's murderer could be lurking among these graves. But that's not what frightened me. Since my husband's illness began, I was much more afraid of what I could see.

Just the week before, Christopher had lain on a smooth, metal table in the Cardiac Center, taped up to a Doppler machine. I sat in a straight-back chair at his feet, our fall jackets slung over my lap like a blanket, clutching a pamphlet called "Do You Know A Blind Person?" It outlined the courtesy rules of blindness. Don't raise your voice or talk to him like a child, it said. Don't grab him by the arm while he is walking. Don't avoid the words "to see." If he is your house guest, show him the bathroom, closet, dresser and window. Let him know whether the lights are on. Only the blind may carry white canes. If you are driving and see a person with a white cane extended beyond the street curb, yield to the right of way.

None of these rules took into account my husband's loss, or my fear of caring for him when complete blindness set in. When the nurse turned off the examination room light and rubbed a Vaseline-coated Doppler over my husband's neck, chest and stomach, I looked rudely inside his body, saw piles of snow-like plaque shoveled against the sides of his carotid artery. His heart became a worn baseball glove, opening and closing inside his chest. Then I saw the fetus, floating blind and sexless in his abdomen. I'd run out of the office to the parking lot to sit in our truck and wait for the nurse to finish with him. A while later, Christopher opened the passenger seat door, slid in beside me.

"Well, that was exciting," he said. "I've never had a woman rub Vaseline over my body while my wife watched."

"I thought I saw a baby in your abdomen," I said.

87

Christopher frowned, took my hand. "I need you to pull yourself together. From now on, you're going to see all kinds of things. You can't imagine babies in my stomach and run out of the doctor's office."

"What should I be doing then?"

"We go on as though none of this is happening."

We sat in the truck for a long time, watching the traffic pass on the street before us. A flock of robins descended on the crooked holly tree beside the truck. As the birds feasted on the late berries, their wings buzzed fiercely, snapping against twigs. Sharp leaves dropped all around us, shattering against the truck's roof and hood. Across the street, the sky was dark violet against the yellow sycamore leaves, and for a moment I forgot why we were sitting in our truck, in the middle of the afternoon, in the middle of the week. This still moment felt sacred, like the weekends we drove until we reached the mountains. For hours, we'd sit side by side on a high, bald rock, watching hundreds of redtail hawks kettling up on the morning thermals, riding the updrafts from the cliffs below us.

As I walked toward the castle, I distracted myself with facts from Donald's afternoon lecture about the castle and its grounds. He'd called this graveyard "the dead center" of Rosslyn; he'd lectured on hawks, explaining how the female was larger, stronger than her edgy mate. I recalled the story of Isis, the sun god's wife who gathered her husband's dismembered body from the Delta banks, reassembling and anointing him until he became whole again, guarding over him in the guise of a hawk. Ashamed of my own fear and weakness, I turned off the flashlight and closed my eyes. Guided only by the sounds of icy gravel crunching beneath my feet, I walked slowly through the darkness until I reached the heavy door and let myself in.

That night, Donald took his place at the head of the table in the green dining room and seated us on either side of him. Margaret circled the table with a tureen, ladling out mussels, shrimp and squid, a clear broth of clam juice and white wine into our deep bowls. Donald held both our hands and delivered the grace.

"Some hae meat an' canna eat an some wad eat that want it. But we hae meat an' we can eat an' sae the Lord be thankit."

When we finished our soup, Margaret took away our empty bowls and brought ice cream drizzled with port. We ate slowly, scraping spoons against metal, pacing ourselves for a meal that would last all evening. Donald served the next course buffet style off the hutch in the library, beside the wall that was covered by a ceiling-high bookshelf filled with books on fencing, cooking and falconry. The basket handled rapier leaned against the mantle of a fireplace that was so big an ox could be roasted inside of it.

Christopher and I stood single file as Donald scooped generous portions of dal, lamb vendaloo and saffron rice onto our plates. After we were seated again, Donald poured the next course of wine and remained standing. He leaned on the table, propping himself up with three fingers, pausing ceremoniously, as though he were about to say another grace. Christopher and I put down our forks, waited for him to speak.

"They were like recalcitrant children," he began, telling us how the Makhabarat guards blind folded him and took him to the red room for questioning. "They cut off frozen sections of hose and beat my bare feet; they pulled out my teeth and fingernails. Once, however, they came for my cellmate and told him they were giving him a birthday party. When they took him away, I thought I'd seen the last of the man, but a few hours later they brought him back. He said that when he arrived in the red room they gave him a cake with candles on it. They sang the 'Happy Birthday' song to him."

"How did you survive it all?" I asked.

"They gave me a single threadbare blanket," he said. "Whenever I found myself dangerously close to self pity, I pulled strands from it and wove them into a noose strong enough to hang myself. I placed the noose above the doorway, where they wouldn't find it. From then on, no matter what those devils did, I knew they couldn't touch me."

Donald was in a holding cell packed with thirty Iraqi prisoners when the guards brought in three American journalists. The other prisoners lifted him over their heads and passed him to the front of the cell. He said he had time to signal them with the letters U.K. before one

89

of the guards knocked him out.

"It took seven weeks for the British Consulate to get me out of prison, and then, on the day of my release, they forgot to reserve a room at the British Embassy suites. While I waited for a hotel vacancy, one of the prison guards drove me around Baghdad. The driver stopped before a copper souk and told me to wait in the back seat of the taxi. He came back with a copper platter and presented it to me, he said, 'in remembrance of our city.' It was gorgeous, the best part of the trip."

Donald disappeared into the library and returned with a large copper platter. Rimmed with egg-sized indentions, it was engraved with half-clad men. Kneeling, they raised their brown, primitive arms to the sun. I didn't know what to say, so I ran my hands over the indentions.

"What would you do if you ever saw one of those guards on the street?" Christopher asked.

"Why, I'd kill him." Donald's eyes were cool, his voice emotionless.

Margaret carried out a crock of doves marinated in red wine vinegar. Donald placed a single dove on each of our plates then served himself. He began eating with his hands, tearing the white meat from the delicate bones, the red vinegar drizzling down his wrists. I couldn't eat. My feet had fallen asleep from sitting still for too long. My eyes burned from not blinking. I wanted to run from the room, but I stayed. Watching the small birds sway in the inky sauce, I remembered Donald's clipped words in the kitchen, This isn't a meal. It's a production. I understood that his story was a gift. He meant to assure us that the body could survive violent loss as long as the mind remained strong. But I took no courage from his words. I felt hostage to his strange blessing.

After a course of cheese and biscuits, then slices of brandied fruit cake, we all retired to the library to sip whiskey and discuss books before the cavernous fireplace.

"It's funny," Donald said. "When I was a lad I'd open up a book to its first page and read its first sentence. Sometimes, the line struck me as so beautiful that I was afraid to read the second. I'd close the book and put it back on the shelf. I wouldn't find that book again for years. Sometimes I'd never find it."

I remembered my own habit of losing books. Whenever I misplaced one, Christopher would tease, "It's gone. It's gone. Somebody must have stolen it." Then he'd go find the book beneath the bed or behind the book shelf and give it back to me. Drowsy with too much wine and food, I closed my eyes and sank inside myself, feeling an unreasonable sadness for lost books.

I heard Donald's voice from across the room, "She looks like the death mask of Nefertiti," and opened my eyes. Embarrassed to be caught sleeping, I excused myself to go to bed, slipped out of the library and wandered toward my room.

There was a castle ghost, of course, a shy one named the White Lady. Donald said that she'd been sighted only once. On Donald's wife's last night in the castle, the white lady had pulled a chair up to the side of her bed and sat, watching over her while she slept. The next morning, Donald's wife had refused to move the chair back to the corner of the room, claiming that someone must have wanted the chair beside the bed and that he'd be wise to leave it. Perhaps it was the strong wine from dinner, or maybe the dull, heavy grief I'd been carrying for the last few weeks had eased, but that night I felt like I was drifting, spectral and unseen, my own skin translucent in the green darkness of the hallway. I could go anywhere in the castle; no one would notice me. I reached the foyer and stood at the foot of the half-decorated pine. Grabbing the thick, gold ribbon from a low branch, I began winding it up and around the tree. Dry needles pricked my skin, falling around my feet. The memory of Donald nodding shyly toward the tree, asking me to decorate it, made me heartsick, guilty for my ungrateful thoughts at the dinner table while he told his story. I remembered the discounted rum and chocolate from the liquor store, decided to wrap them all up for him in the ribbon and place the small gifts Scottish style between the pine branches.

On my way to fetch the gifts, I paused before the red room, taking in the hoarded office equipment.

"Will you be needing some fresh towels, ma'am?"

I startled, so caught up in feeling invisible that I was surprised that Margaret had even seen me.

"No," I said. "Thanks. We haven't used the ones in our room yet."

"You'll be needing some tomorrow, then?"

"Yes. That would be great. Thanks."

Margaret lingered in the doorway, turning on the light in the red room. She went over to the desk, opened a notebook filled with lists of numbers and pound signs, a graph filled with wavy lines. "That is where he keeps track of his wife's travel expenses," she said. I traced the lines with my finger, the curves rising and falling like the Doppler rhythm of a heartbeat, feeling subversive. Margaret tucked a stray hair back into her braid. Her fingers were weathered, startlingly red and chapped against her pale, smooth face. How had such a young woman acquired those old hands?

"We shouldn't be in here," I said, pushing past the girl.

Margaret followed me down the hallway, explaining that Mr. Maclain had sought to make a sensible compromise between due regard for safety and the careful retention of the character of the castle so that it would remain interesting. She cautioned me to watch for steps worn with age and with narrow treads; she warned of uneven surfaces, of low doors and ceiling beams, the dangers of absent lighting in the hallways. If he is your house guest, show him the bathroom, closet, dresser and window, I thought. Let him know whether the lights are on.

When I reached my room, she called after me, "Where shall I put your towels in the morning?"

"Just leave them outside the door," I said, closing the door.

In the guest room, I undressed but couldn't sleep. I wondered why Margaret had shown me those awful accounts of Donald's wife's spending. Had she known about Christopher's blindness? Was she warning me of the unexpected hazards my own husband and I would need to chart and negotiate? Pacing the room, I considered the sketches of the nineteenth century woman that hung one above the other on the white walls. Sketched by a lover who'd caught her off guard, the woman was always alone, lying supine in a lounge chair, or playing the piano or sitting on a stone garden wall, looking down at her hands. In one, she stood bare-shouldered, leaning against a piano, her eyes half closed, the old fashioned gown wrapped around her hips and torso so smooth and sheer it could have been a sheet. Turning away from these tender portraits, I couldn't help feeling as though I'd been looking at something I shouldn't have seen.

I opened the empty drawers beneath the vanity, lifted the silver brush and empty bottle of perfume that were propped on a mirror, dusted myself with stale talcum. In the closet, I filed through a row of tailored cocktail dresses that hung from a low bar, covered with dry cleaning bags above a row of black and beige pumps. It occurred to me that these were the belongings a woman leaves behind when she isn't coming back. The task of caring for Christopher and keeping our marriage in tact suddenly seemed overwhelming. I'd never doubted my own faithfulness to Christopher, but lately I'd become shy with him, ashamed of betraying him with thoughts of my own loss and dread. At that moment, I wanted to leave this sad estate without my husband, flee to some place warm and sunny, like Italy, check into an anonymous inn by the sea, sleep and sleep until the inevitable darkness set in. I felt dangerously close to self pity.

After midnight, Christopher came into the guest room, folded his pants and shirt over the foot of the bed.

"His wife isn't coming back," I said. When Christopher didn't say anything, I added. "How can a woman eat, sleep and make love to a man for years and then leave him one day without telling him she isn't coming back?"

"Maybe it was a long time coming," he said. "You never know what really goes on in someone else's marriage."

"I didn't believe Donald's stories about the prison when he first told me," I said.

Christopher was quiet again. "It doesn't matter if he's telling the truth," he said finally. "He believes what he is saying."

"Why did you choose to tell him about your eye? Why not someone closer, from home?"

"I knew that if something happened to me, he would take care of things."

"Am I one of those things?"

Christopher closed his eyes. I studied his profile, the nose that had been broken by a football, the broad cheekbones, the first silver hair curling through his beard. I knew these features better than my own, and though I'd never intended for it to be this way, I'd grown used to measuring all my feelings by what I saw in his face. I wondered if it were the same for him, and how our love would change once he no longer could see me.

I placed my hand over his good eye.

"What do you see?" I asked.

"I see the top of your head and the bottom of your chin. The rest of your face is missing."

I dropped my hand from his eye, sad desire rising within my chest, spreading through my arms and legs. There was no time to reach for the condoms I'd thrown hopefully into the bottom of my cosmetic bag, no time for soft kisses or lingering hands. I couldn't explain my own selfish recklessness, or stop it. I knew only that I wanted my husband as close as possible, with nothing between us. Suddenly, his breath caught, startling us both, and we broke apart. When he rolled over, I curved myself around his back, covering him with my body, placing my foot between his calves. He rolled gently away from me, pulled up the sheets we'd kicked to the foot of the bed, and flipped on the white noise machine. My whole body ached for him, but I was afraid to touch him again.

"Donald wants to take us hawking in the morning," he said. "Better try and get some rest."

Sounds of running water filled the bedroom, but I could hear a rhythmic tick beneath the noise machine's false current. When I turned it off, Christopher said nothing. We listened to the pigeons brooding beneath the eaves outside our window, the churning forest around us. The lonely scent of Donald's pine tree remained on my hands and in my hair, spreading through the bed. Though I didn't think it was possible, I fell into a deep and senseless sleep.

I awoke to the sound of china cups clanking against their saucers down in the kitchen. The chilled bedroom air smelled of old fires, hot tea. Outside the bare window, the hawthorn branches were black against the white morning sky. I rose, dressed quickly and walked down to the yellow kitchen.

Donald stood before the gas range, stirring porridge, a dish towel slung over his shoulder. A draft blew beneath the kitchen door and over my bare toes.

"He's still asleep," I said.

Donald handed me the porridge spoon, instructing me to stir while he poured hot water over the tea leaves in each cup. I felt the same impulse to dispense with the small talk, my own shameless need to confide in him. Donald turned off the fire, moving the porridge on the back burner. He wiped his hands on the dish towel, looking steadily at me.

"Tell me about your wife," I said.

"The first time I brought Marion to Rosslyn, I saw a band of shoe string licorice in a shop window down in the village, and she told me she hadn't seen candy like that since she was a girl. I ran into the shop and bought it for her, but she wouldn't eat it. When I asked why, she said, 'I've always hated black licorice.' Then she told me she was going back to Wales."

"Did she explain why?"

"When I was in prison, the British Consulate told her I was dead. I suppose she planned the next ten years of her life without me. Once I was home, I suppose she couldn't see things any other way."

"Have you asked her to come home?"

"Marion is Welsh. When a Welsh woman makes up her mind to do something, there is no discussion."

"Christopher and I used to talk about everything. He was the first man I'd ever met who could hold up his end of a conversation. I think that's why I married him. What scares me the most right now is all this quietness between us."

It seemed that once I started, I couldn't stop talking to this lonely man. I voiced the pent-up fears that had kept me frozen, suspended for

95

the last several weeks. At first, I hadn't believed Christopher was going blind. The day it started, I'd found him sitting at the dining room table with his head in his hands. He'd been vacuuming, he said, and when he bent over to pick up a sock beneath our bed, everything went black in his right eye, as though a cloud had shifted over his vision. Confused and angry, I nearly accused him of faking it to get out of housework.

"I don't blame him for resenting me," I said. "But he has it all wrong. He thinks I won't love him anymore once he's blind. He thinks that if he keeps his illness from me, I won't stop loving him. The truth is whenever I've compared Christopher to other men—no matter how strong and healthy—they are the ones who seem… deficient." I stopped. We both understood what I couldn't say: if something happened to my husband, there could be no one else.

Donald opened the kitchen door, went to the hall closet and tossed a barbour jacket and a pair of boots to me.

"Put these on," he said, opening the back door. "Come with me."

The cliffs beneath the cottage were drilled with low caves, guarded by warped chain-linked fences. It was said that William Wallace had once hidden in them, that the villagers who once lived in the glen had called them "dungeons." Donald now stored his wine and bird hutch in them. He unlocked the padlock of the lowest dungeon, and we walked into the dusty light, stepping over the stone rubble on the floor. Donald gathered a leash, hood and traveling perch from the cave-like oven in the far wall. Then he moved toward the heated wooden hutch.

Isis was a young bird, born into captivity, accustomed to sultry Texas heat. More troubled by the cold than I, she flew out of her hutch and outside the cave. We followed her, watching her land on a pine limb 30 yards above us, refusing to fly down. Donald went back into the castle and returned with a handful of raw stew beef, holding up his calf-skin glove. The hawk finally rotated over our heads, dropped, and Donald's arm dipped like a thin branch beneath the force of her landing. Tall and slender, the bird's black feathers hooded her head and chestnut wings like a cape. She devoured the raw meat, then stood uneasily, panting, bobbing her head back and forth, those fierce black eyes searching the pines behind us. Donald paused, as though chastening himself, before gently coaxing her onto his fist.

We crossed the bridge above the North Esk, following the river along a path lined with clumps of snowberries until we reached a clearing that stretched for half a mile, ending in a thicket. Black-faced sheep grazed on a distant foothill, and the shadows of clouds swept quickly across the frozen field like giant, dark wings. Donald explained that our chief concern as falconers was learning how to put all our trust into an animal that could disappear over the horizon in fifteen seconds flat. He said some breeds of falcons could feel the pulse of their prey, reach into its body and squeeze the life out of its heart. The Harris hawk shattered its victim's skull on impact or inserted its curved beak inside the vertebrae, snapping the spine.

When Donald pulled his arm back, the hawk blinked, ruffled her feathers and shook them down. Donald swung his arm forward, casting the hawk into the air. She rose, teetering on the frail wind, her delicate wing feathers brushing the cold air like fingers. As she circled, flapping and gliding, he released the ferret into one of the burrows, and a jackrabbit crashed out of its cover, heading for the thicket. The hawk folded her wings, dropped, missing the rabbit just as it reached the thicket.

As we walked farther into the clearing, the hawk recovered, following us in the air. Donald called down the bird.

"I'd like to try," I said.

He nodded, handed the extra glove to me. I pulled the glove on and made a fist. Donald transferred the hawk to my arm, and I felt her talons pinch and hold while she grabbed for the meat on my hand. Once fed, she preened beneath her wings, her brown and black feathers spreading and shifting like muddy currents of water, the tiny bells around her leg jingling. I pulled my arm back, casting her into the air, waiting. She flew higher, becoming a black speck in the white sky, vanishing. I felt breathless, full of wonder and panic.

"She's gone," I said. "I've lost your bird."

"Wait," Donald said.

A flock of starlings flew in, diving together, turning in such perfect synchronicity that they disappeared on the horizon for a moment, then reappeared in the same shape. The hawk appeared, wind screaming through the bells on her leg as she dropped to the earth like a stone. She slammed into a starling, flew through the explosion of feathers, struck again and again. Binding herself to her quarry, she carried it down from the sky and perched like a goddess on a limb above me, so close I could see her bloody talons.

I stood below her, feeling ungrounded, the guilt and strain of the last month draining completely from my arms and legs, into the crystallized leaves beneath my feet. I let go of my violent urge to flee from the sickness that would wear away at Christopher and me until we no longer recognized ourselves. I knew only that these changes were inevitable, that we must cling to each other through the flurry of our new emotions. The hawk was waiting for me to approach, but I turned from her, made my way back to the castle, where my husband still slept in the bed where I'd left him. I wanted to wake him up. I wanted to show him all that I had seen.